CHOOSE THE BEAR

IN THE WILD

BOOK ONE

LAUREN SMITH

ISBN: 978-1-962760-66-9 (e-book edition)

ISBN: 978-1-962760-67-6 (paperback edition)

AUTHOR'S NOTE

Dear lovely reader,

Thank you for choosing the bear. If you have not heard the recent question that surfaced on various social media platforms about 'choosing the bear' then let me briefly explain the origins of this story and my intentions in writing it.

A question was posed to women all over the world: Would you rather be stranded in the woods with a bear or a man? The vast majority of women replied that they would choose the bear. The bear would likely avoid them and in general the woman would be far safer than if she faced a man. Naturally men all over the world were stunned to hear this. But we women understand the truth, the worst a bear could do was kill us, but a man? There are a thousand things worse than death which a woman could suffer at the hand of a dangerous man.

We know that not all men are bad, but as women, we face the fact that our lives are not as safe simply because we are women. We travel with our car keys between our fingers, we lock all of our doors and triple check those locks, we alert our girl friends when we go out on dates as to where we will be and what our date looks like. We take a thousand precautions because we must.

When I set out to write this book, I had one goal in mind. I wanted to paint the truth of what a woman goes through during an assault by a man she knows (women are far more likely to be attacked by a domestic partner, than a stranger). I wanted to show how a strong, smart, independent woman could lose herself in a relationship and not see the danger signs until it was too late.

I know that this may be a triggering or sensitive subject. The first chapter is perhaps the hardest in the story, but important not to ignore. I have done my best to make the worst part as quick as possible. The rest of the story is about healing from such an attack emotionally not just physically. Hadlee, my heroine learns what it means to meet a truly good man, a man who will always do what is right for her, will always respect her and give her what she wants and needs.

In many ways this is a standard paranormal romance with a shifter hero, but I hope you'll find something important within these pages that reminds you that you have incredible value to the world, that you are beautiful, you are brilliant, and that you can save yourself because you are the heroine of your own life story.

This is my love letter to you dear reader. You are not alone, you are a woman and we build our lives around community. When women come together, we possess infinite strength and infinite compassion.

So if you ever face a man in the woods...just remember you don't have to choose the bear...*you can be the bear.*

~Lauren Smith, September 2024

1

It wasn't supposed to end like this...

Hadlee Wilson scrambled through the under-brush deep in woods deep of the Colorado mountains and ducked behind a tree, crouching down to hide. For a moment all was silent around her, except for the soft whisper of the breeze through the aspen trees and an occasional bird twittering far above her. But all of that was drowned out by the pounding of the blood in her ears as she tried to remember how to breathe.

Tears blurred her eyes, and she clamped her hand over her mouth to stifle a sob. Was this how her life was going to end? Being assaulted and murdered in the woods by Chad, her boyfriend?

She desperately tried to think back over the last six months. What signs had she missed? Chad Parker had seemed *perfect*. He was handsome, single, and had a good job. Everyone who met him liked him. He had showered her with gifts from the day they'd met, and this wasn't the first trip they'd taken together. So what had changed? Had she done something to make him angry enough to—

Her thoughts careened to a halt and her instincts took over as she heard footsteps approaching. It sounded like hiking boots crunching leaves and snapping twigs. Soft, but definitely moving in her direction.

"Hadlee..." Chad's voice was almost polite, almost pleasant, but she heard a hint of a sneer lurking in the way he said her name. "We talked about this, babe. I told you men have needs. You can't freak out over a little bit of choking, okay?"

Hadlee's hand reached up to touch her bruised throat. If she survived this, there would be a black circle around her neck in the shape of Chad's hands. He'd gotten too rough, too quickly for her. She'd thought she might like it when he first put his hands on her throat in a possessive but gentle hold while they made love. But seconds later, he'd squeezed *hard*. He hadn't paid attention when she'd started to blackout and clawed at his fingers. She breathlessly begged him to stop, but he'd only laughed at her. When black spots danced before her eyes, she knew she'd made a terrible mistake. She liked rough sex sometimes, but Chad hadn't just been rough. He'd been *brutal.* Homicidal. It wasn't fun, but rather terrifying when he'd started to slap her and then punched her skull. Then he tore her shirt and tried to undo her jeans. She'd fought him, despite the blinding pain in her head. She'd kicked and clawed and somehow gotten free to run into the woods. But he'd still found her...

"You don't even know where the hell you are, bitch." Chad's voice sounded hardened. "Why do you think I blindfolded you? It wasn't for romance, *babe.*" He snarled out a laugh.

Every breath that escaped her was too loud. She covered her mouth with her hands, trying to stifle the sound.

"If you don't come out now, I will leave you here and you'll die in the woods. If you get eaten by a bear, serves you right," he spat.

At this point, Hadlee would have gladly chosen death by bear. All the creature would do was kill her. Whatever Chad had in mind for her ... would be far worse than death. She held still, continuing to hunker down against the large tree and prayed she'd hear his footfalls grow quieter as he moved away.

Silence.

She didn't dare move. In every horror movie she'd

ever seen, the woman thought she was safe and left her hiding spot, which always revealed her location to the homicidal maniac. There was no damn way she was going to do that. She'd stay right where she was for the rest of her life if it kept her alive.

Suddenly Chad's face peered around the tree that she was hiding behind and she screamed. His brown eyes were lit with demonic fire. Pure terror exploded through her chest, and she couldn't even scream, let alone breathe.

He lunged at her, his fingers digging into her hair and wrenching her head toward him as she tried to escape. He punched her in the face with his other hand and pain exploded around her left eye. She crumpled, a wail slipping from her lips as the pain worsened.

"That's it, scream, bitch! No one will hear you." Chad threw her to the ground. Kicks rained down on her and it felt like one of her ribs cracked.

Fight.

The single word broke through the stabbing agony fogging her mind.

Fight!

A sudden surge of adrenaline shot through her. She rammed an elbow into his throat as he bent down. Something crunched beneath where she'd hit him, and he choked out a sound of agony. Without another glance back, she ran. It didn't matter to where, anywhere was safer.

Something hot and wet dripped down her face and she wiped frantically at her nose. When she lifted her hand up, she saw blood smeared over her fingers. The blood dripped onto the leaves and plants at her feet as she fled.

Oh God, could he track her blood trail? Terrified at the thought she was leaving a path for him to follow, she ran recklessly now, taking every leap and springing step she could, desperate to put distance between her and Chad before she found another place to hide.

"Ahh!" She barreled straight over a ledge that dropped suddenly, and she plummeted fifteen feet into a stream. Something twisted sharply in her ankle, and she landed face down in the shallow water. The cold stream felt like ice, but she welcomed the numbness of her face. She lifted her head to breathe. Water rushed around her in little swirling eddies as she pushed herself up a few more inches.

Have to keep moving. Can't stop, the voice in her head said again. *Keep moving!* The voice practically bellowed at her. The words were deep, insistent, and tinged with fear. Her inner voice had never sounded like that before. She tried to breathe, her lungs straining against the broken rib. and all she could draw in was a raspy inhalation.

Was she dying? That must be it. Her inner voice no longer sounded as it should because she wasn't getting enough oxygen for her brain to work.

Come on, honey, you need to move, her inner voice begged her.

She dug her hands into the mud and dragged herself up to her hands and knees, despite how much it hurt.

"Such a pity." Chad's voice came from behind her. "Everyone back at the office will be devastated to hear that you had an accident and fell just after I proposed to you. I didn't have time to put the ring on your finger. You turned and looked out over the incredible view and slipped... You fell down a ravine and broke every bone in your stupid little body." He was telling himself a crazy story, his tone gleeful. Hadlee kept moving, even if it was just a few inches at a time. She refused to look back at him.

Pain dug its claws into her spine as Chad stomped a boot on her lower back and crushed her back into the stream.

He leaned over her and whispered, "Don't you get it, Hadlee? You caused this. Were you stupid enough to think I actually want you? That I gave a fuck about you?

You're just another dumb bitch who deserves everything I'm about to do to you."

The fire to fight, which had burned so hot within her, died out, leaving her weak, cold, shivery. She couldn't move, couldn't get him off her. He was simply too strong. Her body gave up a second later, every muscle sinking into the rushing stream and mud-covered stone bank beneath her.

Hadlee's face was wet with blood and water as she lifted her head with the last of her waning strength. If she was going to die, she wanted to see the trees and the sky one last time. The thick foliage formed a pattern of silvery veins, branches fanning out so the trees could touch each other. The leaves rippled in the breeze, sounding like waves washing upon a beach. It was peaceful. But she was so tired ... so very tired, and as her head dropped toward the ground, that was when she saw it.

A bear. A massive grizzly bear stood downstream, its muzzle dripping with water. It was staring at her.

"Help me ... *please...*" she whispered, knowing how very stupid it was to beg a wild animal to help her.

The bear's golden-brown eyes continued to watch her.

"What the fuck?" Chad's boot lifted off her back. "That's a fucking bear! Now you're going to die, you bitch!" She glanced over her shoulder to see Chad sprinting up the slope and running back the way they'd come.

The bear raised its head to the sky, opened its jaws, and roared. A second later, the bear began loping toward her.

This is it. This is how I die...

Hadlee covered her head with her hands and held still as it thundered directly at her, his paws rumbling the earth with their impact. She felt a rush of air above her and a hard, shaking blow to the ground behind her.

Chad screamed in the distance, then the sound abruptly cut off and the woods were silent except for the faint gurgle of the stream. Hadlee heard the grunting pants of the bear as it came back to her.

Play dead. Wasn't that what she'd heard on some documentary? Most bears would leave you alone, right? But wait, that was black bears. This wasn't a black bear but a grizzly. Was that the one you were supposed to run like hell from? She tried to remember, but her thoughts spiraled over and over in her mind like a kaleidoscope until she felt like she would throw up.

A snout nudged her knee, and she flinched but she forced herself to hold still. There were soft splashes by her face and she peered between two fingers covering her eyes to see the bear washing its bloody jaws off in the stream. Red blood blended with the crystalline waters as it moved past her downstream.

That was Chad's blood. It had to be. A chill rippled along her spine when she realized she would be next. But at least the end would be swift. The bear wouldn't torture her. The creature huffed and splashed his paws in the water before turning to look at her. Its head tilted slightly, and it made a snorting sort of sound, as if deeply breathing in the air to scent her.

She tried to stare back at the bear, but the pain in her body was too much to tolerate any longer. It was harder and harder to pull her thoughts together, to make sense of anything. Her consciousness began to slip, and she blinked, slower and slower. Just before her eyes closed for the final time, she thought she saw a shape far too small to be a bear coming toward her ... and then she blacked out.

INDIANA RIVERS STARED AT THE INJURED WOMAN LYING HALF out of the stream. She was unconscious now. His blood still pounded in his ears as his body finished the last part of the physical change. The remnants of the bear receded and left the man part of him behind. He curled his hands into fists and stared at the woman, then glanced at the woods over his shoulder.

The human male was dead. One good bite and Indiana had torn the man's throat open. The memory of killing the male was sharp and clear, like all the things he saw and experienced when in his bear form, but unlike the other memories he had when he changed, this was not a memory he wanted to keep. He wasn't a killer, at least not of men. But just moments ago, he'd taken a life to save this woman. A woman he didn't even know. Yet he would have done the same for any female in danger, without thought or hesitation.

Crouching down, Indiana put his arms around the woman and lifted her from the water. She was soaking wet, and the scent of her blood was sickly sweet in his nose. As he carried her through the woods, he tried to make sense of what it just happened. He had been in his bear form for less than an hour, prowling as he usually did on his lands, taking in the scent of the fall leaves on the breeze.

But less than ten minutes ago, he'd started feeling strange things. A panic in his chest, an erratic flash of images in his head of the forest, and he'd felt the wild urge to fight, to strike out at what was making him panic. He'd never felt so … out of control and unlike himself before.

Trying to clear his head, he'd made his way to the little stream that ran through part of his land. He'd only taken a few licks of water when he'd heard a frightened animal tearing through the forest, coming in his direction. He'd waited, unmoving, that hard pounding of fear still in his chest even though it hadn't felt quite like his own fear. And that was when he'd seen the human female fall down the embankment and crash into the water. She'd lain there but seconds before a human male followed her down into the stream and continued the attack he'd clearly started somewhere else. Indiana had stood frozen, stunned by seeing something so vicious occurring on his land right before his eyes. His gaze had locked with the woman's as she'd stared at him.

"Help me…" she'd pleaded. The breeze carried her broken words to him and the shock that had kept him still spurred him into motion. A primal rage had exploded through him, demanding justice. He had killed that male for daring to harm a precious female. Bear shifter clans fiercely respected and revered females for their bravery and strength, and to attack one, even a human female, was an unforgiveable crime. So he'd slain the man before he could stop himself.

And now I'm in deep shit, he thought.

There was a dead body on his land, and he held a very badly injured woman in his arms whom he was now responsible for. What the hell was he going to do?

His cabin wasn't far, about two miles away, and at a steady walking pace he would reach it within half an hour. He had that long to figure out what to do.

He was still debating his options when he finally climbed the steps of his front porch. With a practiced adeptness, he carefully adjusted his hold on the woman so he could use two fingers to press the numbered keypad on his door and open it. A low, cheery *woof* greeted him and he spotted his rescued mutt, Jones, waiting for him in the entryway. The dog was some kind of crossbreed between a golden retriever and a sheepdog, if Indiana had to guess. He'd found the dog on the side of the road, abandoned and half-starved. He'd lured Jones into his care with a bit of a leftover hamburger from his lunch, and they'd been the best of friends ever since.

"Now go easy on our new friend, Jones," he told the dog, and Jones huffed happily and wagged his tail so hard the back half of his body wiggled back and forth. Indiana wasn't much of a people person and like many bear shifters, preferred to be alone. Jones, however, couldn't get enough of people, especially women and children.

Indiana carried the woman to the brown leather couch in his den on the first floor and laid her down. He would tend to her wounds immediately after he had a chance to get pants on. The last thing this poor woman needed was to wake up while the huge naked man examined her injuries.

"Jones, watch our guest," he commanded. The mutt sat down by the couch and gave the woman a curious sniff, his tail slowly swishing around.

Certain she would be fine for a few minutes, Indiana went to his bedroom and then into the master shower, quickly rinsing off the blood and dirt from his skin and hair. He toweled off and pulled on a pair of jeans and a dark-green T-shirt. He paused only to check his reflection, which he hardly ever did because the scarred face looking back at him always soured his mood. The long scar across his cheek and throat were white now, but his body still flinched at the memory of being attacked by a mountain lion when he'd been a young cub.

Christ, the woman would take one look at him and probably faint dead away. Something in his chest twinged, and he rubbed at the spot just above his heart at the pang of unexpected longing he felt. It was his struggle, his burden. As a bear shifter without a clan, he hadn't found a mate among his people. He couldn't risk having a human female as mate, let alone a lover, because what human could he trust with the beast side of his soul? Could any human even be trusted to keep his secret? He could never have a normal life, could never pretend he was just like everyone else. With a low growl, he walked back into the den and found Jones still watching the sleeping woman with the patient, keen interest only dogs were capable of.

"Still out, eh?" he asked the dog, and gave Jones a scratch behind his ears.

Jones whined softly and his tail thumped against the floor.

Indiana left the den again and retrieved the large red box that held his first aid supplies from the hall closet. He sat down on the edge of the ottoman in front of the couch and removed antiseptic wipes, gauze, antibacterial cream, and band-aids. He knew the second he touched her with the antiseptic cloths, she would probably feel the intense burn which would make her wake up and scream. So he paused for a couple of seconds to just look at her, because it might be his only chance before the screaming and panicking started.

The woman was about five foot four inches, with

curves that made his hands itch to touch. She had beautiful russet-colored hair bound up in a loose ponytail, which had come partially undone during her fall into the stream. She was lovely in a girl-next-door sort of way. There was something about her that made his inner bear want to stare at her forever and to rip apart the human who'd dare to harm her. Which he'd done…

"You ready, boy?" he asked Jones as he opened the pouch of antiseptic wipes. Indiana leaned over the woman, braced his elbows on his knees, and wiped at a large scrape on her leg. The woman's nostrils flared and her eyes flew open, revealing a lovely shade of green. She stared at him and a second later she screamed. His overly sensitive ears took in the shriek, and he winced. A second later, a hard little fist punched his jaw. It didn't hurt much, because he was a lot harder to wound than a human, but he was surprised at the woman's strength given how hurt she was.

The woman curled back in on herself, clutching her wrist as she heaved sobs and tried to protect herself. The sight broke his heart.

"Easy, honey," Indiana soothed. "You're safe now. The man who attacked you is dead." It was probably too abrupt to drop the facts on her like that, but if he'd been in her position, that news would put him at ease.

Her wide green eyes fixed on his as she tried to speak between panting sobs.

"He's ... he's dead?" She finally got the words out. Her body trembled hard enough that the floor shook in faint vibrations, which Indiana felt beneath his bare feet.

"Yeah."

"Was it ... was it the bear?" she asked.

Indiana debated his options, but decided to stick to simple truths.

"Yes, a bear killed him. And I need to call the sheriff and lead him to the body."

She mouthed the words "the body," and her gaze drifted into the distance. Shock was setting in.

"Honey, what's your name?" he asked as he once more cleaned her scrapes. She flinched but let him wipe blood away from the wounds and bandage them up.

"It's Hadlee ... Hadlee Wilson."

"Hadlee, I'm Indiana, and this is Jones." He nodded at the dog. She focused more sharply on him, suspicion flashing in her green eyes.

"Indiana and Jones? How can you joke at a time like this? I—"

"I'm not joking. My parents named me Indiana, and when I got this old bag of bones, well, he looked like a

Jones. Trust me, the irony of the situation is not lost on me."

She pinched her nose, then winched when she seemed to realize it was tender and closed her eyes as she blew out a long sigh. "This is a dream, isn't it?"

"Afraid not." Indiana set the first aid kit to one side and cupped her chin, wiping the blood from the base of her nose and around her lips. He went on to clean her cheeks and brow. Her dark lashes fluttered as tears escaped her eyes.

"Hey now," he murmured, and brushed the tears away with the pads of his thumbs.

She sniffled and her lashes flew up as she gazed at him again. "You are really named Indiana?" she asked, her words tremulous. So that was the thing she was focusing on over everything else? If it hadn't been such a serious moment, he would have laughed.

"That's so ridiculous." She started to laugh a little hysterically. "Do I call you Indy or something?"

"You wouldn't be the first. You can call me whatever you want, honey." He rubbed some antibiotic cream on the scrapes on her face. "Now sit tight while I get some ice packs for your ankle and your wrist."

He stood up but she reached out, grasping his hand to stop him.

"Thank you for finding me. I didn't think that I'd ... that I get away," she whispered.

Her words cut him deep. He hadn't been the man to hurt her, but the truth was, many women didn't get away. He knew the statistics of murder and assault on women were too damned high. The bear within him growled low, craving the blood of any male who dared harm a female.

He cleared his throat. "But you did get away, Hadlee. That's what matters." God, he wished he could tell her how lucky he'd been to find her before that male finished what he'd started. But Indiana didn't want her thinking anymore about what had almost happened. It wouldn't help her to heal. He knew all too well what it was like trying to heal not just physically but emotionally after an attack. His had been nothing compared to hers, but he'd still fought for his life all the same.

As he walked into the kitchen, his heart sank as he felt the invisible barriers he had to erect between them. She could never know *he* had been the bear in the woods, that he'd been the one to kill to protect her. She'd be terrified, she'd tell other humans. She would put him in danger. But for now, he was going to take care of her as best he could and when she was ready, he'd have to let her go.

2

Hadlee hurt everywhere, but the pain was secondary to her confusion. Where was she and who the hell was that massive mountain of a man named Indiana? The question which burned deeper than all the rest... Was Chad really dead? Had the bear killed him?

She jumped as a cold wet nose nudged her knee and she glanced down to see the dog he called Jones watching her with a soft, understanding pair of brown eyes. She held out her hand to let him sniff her and when he licked her fingers, she knew it was safe to stroke his head and scratch behind his ears. He really was a pretty dog and definitely some sort of golden retriever mix. She adored dogs. Chad hadn't. He'd always complained about her neighbors dogs when he came over to her place.

Oh God ... Chad's dead.

That bombshell kept falling on her over and over again. She suddenly felt ill. She covered her mouth and leapt up from the couch, only to cry out in pain as her ankle twinged sharply and she vomited on the nice leather sofa.

No, no, no...

"Hadlee?" Indiana was at her side an instant later. He had moved so fast she hadn't even seen him coming. Where had he been?

"Sorry," she groaned miserably. He scooped her up into his arms as though she weighed nothing at all.

"It's easy to clean," he said, his voice gentle. "I'll put you in bed and I'll clean it up. Then I need to call the sheriff."

"No, thank you ... I'm okay. I'm just going to ... leave now." She tried to push against his chest, but he was as immovable as a mountain.

"Aspen Falls, the nearest town, is twenty minutes away by car. I can drive you, but not right now. You need to rest, and we need to stay near the scene unless the Sheriff clears you to go straight to the clinic. Until then, I want you resting in bed."

"Bed?" She tensed in his hold. She didn't think he'd

hurt her or try anything, but after what had happened with Chad, she didn't trust anyone anymore … not even herself.

"I have a guest bedroom you can use." He walked through his house, and she took in the lovely cabin's feel. Part of her was still in shock, she knew it. But she was too tired and too hurt to find the strength to scream or cry in wild hysterics.

"Just let me go … I'll wait outside. I—"

"You're safe here," Indiana murmured, his deep rumbling voice moving out from his chest and into her body in a way which comforted her beyond words. "I imagine you will have trouble believing that, but I promise you it's true."

She didn't reply, she just relaxed a little more against him and focused on examining his home. The structure was all exposed beams and stonework. The space was utterly masculine but also felt cozy and welcoming. The guest bedroom he took her to had a four-poster bed with a white comforter and plush pillows. A dark-green blanket draped over the end of the bed, giving it a splash of woodsy color. Two tall balcony doors were made entirely of glass and the other walls had large photographs of the woods, making it feel like she was still in the forest. That should have bothered her, but the woods didn't scare her. Chad did … and Chad was dead.

"This okay?" Indiana asked.

"Yeah, this is beautiful." She thought of her apartment back in Chicago. It was modern and pretty, but it didn't feel like this. This room was spacious, but she didn't feel lost in it. She studied the view through the balcony doors. The distant mountains hovered just beyond like silent sentries, watchful, protective. Something anxious in her suddenly calmed, like a wave at a beach washing over her feet as she sat down in the sand. She was safe here.

Her heartbeat slowed, matching the steady *thump —thump* of Indiana's heart, which pounded so steadily against her cheek as he cradled her in his arms. It would be a pity when he set her down, so she didn't dare move, in case he thought she wanted him to stop holding her.

"There's a guest bathroom over there in case you need it, but you can't take a shower yet," he said, his brows knit together with sympathy.

"Why not?" She was covered with blood, dirt, and God knew what else.

"You were assaulted by that man. The authorities will need to take pictures of your injuries and make note of defensive wounds. They'll also do a rape kit at the clinic."

"Rape? No, I stopped him before... Wait, how did you know I was assaulted?" She lifted her gaze up to his, searching his face. His golden-brown eyes were that perfect color of honey that drizzled from the combs of a beehive.

"I heard you scream. I was walking near the stream and saw you fall down the embankment. I saw him attack you when you were in the water." He paused. "Then I saw that grizzly bear run past you, chase the man down, and kill him."

"Oh." So he'd seen the bear.

"Hadlee, who was that man? Was he stranger who followed you on the trail while you were hiking?" Indiana asked.

"He was my boyfriend," she whispered. A swell of shame choked her throat and prevented her from speaking further. No matter what she knew she was *supposed* to think and feel, she couldn't shake the guilt. The feeling that she'd been a fool to go camping with Chad and agree to try things he'd wanted try, because those choices had put her in this horrifying situation.

"Why don't you lie down a rest for a bit. I'll wake you when the sheriff is here."

She couldn't speak, and just nodded. After a moment, he walked out of the room and closed the door behind him, leaving her alone. As much as she wanted to sleep, she didn't want to ruin his beautiful white bed with blood and dirt, so she opened the French doors and stepped out onto the deck. There were two Adirondack chairs waiting for people to sit in them. She chose the nearest one, limping over to it and easing down. Every muscle ached and every bone pulsed with pain, but her heartbeat was slow and steady. She drew in a shaky breath and stared at the forest, her mind blissfully shutting down for a long while.

When a hand touched her shoulder, she jolted awake. When had she fallen asleep?

"Hey Hadlee, the sheriff is here along with the coroner and a few other law enforcement officers. They need to take pictures of your wounds and take your statement." Indiana was leaning over her, his handsome face somber as he studied her. He stroked his thumb over Hadlee's shoulder. She shouldn't want a massive man touching her, but *his* touch soothed her. He was so *big* ... far bigger than Chad and he could hurt her ... *kill* her. But while she saw how strong he was, felt it each time his arms came around her, she didn't sense the darkness beneath his skin, the *sickness* she'd felt from Chad over the last few months.

She stared up into his gorgeous honey-brown eyes. She thought she glimpsed silver glints just behind the brown. Faint scars cut across his cheek and throat, but there was no denying he was *beautiful* in that rugged way only a man can be. Even with his hair, which was a tad long and a bit shaggy. He looked *good*. He was not perfectly polished like Chad—that man couldn't stand to have a single hair out of place or a wrinkle in his shirt. Funny, those obsessions hadn't mattered to him at all when he'd attacked her.

"Why are you asleep in the chair?" He glanced around, his brows lowering as if he were troubled.

"I..." She let out a bone-weary sigh. "I'm covered in blood and God knows what else. I didn't want to make anything dirty."

"It's just a bed." His voice was almost a growl with frustration. "I can wash the sheets."

She bit her bottom lip, then winced as she felt an open wound where her lip had split.

"You okay?" Indiana asked, then seemed to reproach himself. "Fuck, of course you're not. I'm not very good at this, am I?"

"Good at what?" she asked when she tried to stand. Her ankle twinged sharply and she cursed as she leaned against the chair for support. Indiana studied her face and caught her by the waist with his large palms.

"I don't spend a lot of time around people," he admitted as he dragged a hand through his hair and glanced away. "I forget the basic skills, you know?"

"I think you are good at it," she argued. "I probably should be having a full-blown panic attack but you've somehow kept me calm."

He raised one dark-brown brow. "Really?"

"Yeah, I definitely would have stroked out hours ago from the stress, but I'm okay." It was true, she was prone to panic and anxiety attacks. Chad used to berate her for it when she started to spiral out.

"That could be the shock," Indiana said as he frowned. Somehow the intense expression on such an attractive, almost intimidating, face was adorable.

She nearly smiled, but her cheeks felt like they were made of shattered glass. Every muscle hurt, even her jaw and cheekbones knifed with pain each time she spoke.

"If you feel up to it, the sheriff is ready to take your statement. The sooner you do that, the quicker you can shower and rest."

She followed him through the bedroom and down the hall. She heard the voices of several men before she saw them. The three men were speaking in low tones. Their vehicles were parked out front and clearly visible through the windows of Indiana's living room.

"Here she is, Sheriff Wade," Indiana announced as they stepped into the main room.

The men all turned and their expressions darkened at the sight of her.

"Jesus Christ," one of them muttered. "It looks like he used her face for a fucking punching bag."

"Shut up, Clive," said an older man. The sheriff, she guessed. He smacked the shoulder of the man who had spoken, and stepped forward to introduce himself more respectfully.

"Ms. Wilson, I'm Sheriff Wade. These are my deputies, Clive and Reeves. I'm sorry I don't have any female officers you could speak with. I can call another police station that might have one, but the closest one would probably be a good hour away. Or I can have a female nurse from our clinic come down to see you."

"It's okay, thank you for asking. I don't need a female officer or nurse." It would be nice to talk to a woman, but she didn't want to delay giving her statement any longer.

"Very well, why don't we take a seat at the kitchen table." Sheriff Wade nodded at a room behind him. She caught a glimpse of white granite countertops and pale French-blue cabinets.

"Okay." She followed the sheriff into the kitchen.

When she and the sheriff were seated at a dark

cherrywood table, mugs of coffee and tea in their hands thanks to Indiana, she told the sheriff everything that had happened, starting from the moment she and Chad had parked their car in the hiking lot and gone up to spend the night in a meadow that was supposed to be good for star gazing. She continued her account up to the moment she blacked out after seeing the bear charge Chad. She kept her story short, talking quickly, and it helped her feel detached, like it had happened to someone else, not her. Somehow that kept the numbness cloaked around her.

"So this Chad Parker was your fiancé?"

Her mind swirled with the rush of thoughts she'd had before she and Chad had come on this trip, how she'd suspected he planned to propose, that this would have been a romantic weekend ... and how wrong she'd been about all of it, about *him*.

"He never asked me ... so I guess ... not."

The sheriff grunted and took some notes, his silvery brows lowered.

As she answered more questions, she felt the soothing presence of Indiana standing just behind her, and his heat. Jones sat beneath the table, leaning his head against her knee, and she patted him every now and then when she felt she needed the reassurance.

"Had Parker ever hit you before?" Sheriff Wade asked. "Or committed any other kind of abuse?"

"No. I mean not physically." But she thought about all the small things—red flags she'd missed. He'd always turned everything they talked about into an argument. If she did anything great at work, he would say that her company had low standards. He never liked the meals she cooked, and he left her to do most of the chores when she was at his place. She was always washing dishes or doing his laundry. Looking back on it, she felt exhausted and unhappy every time she was around him.

From the minute she'd met Parker, he had loved bombed her with gifts and fancy trips. But at the end of the day, being around him had depleted her energy and *depressed* her. Wasn't being in love supposed to lift you up? Make you feel like you could fly? It wasn't supposed to leave you in a constant state of unhappiness; nothing was worth being berated just so you didn't have to be alone. She would have given anything to be alone if it had meant avoiding this trip because it almost cost her her life.

"So the assault began when he tried to initiate sex?"

She nodded. "I was technically consenting at the time, but then he started choking me." Of course consenting was a vague word in that scenario; when someone didn't want to have sex, when did it cross the line to non-consent? She had stopped enjoying sex with Parker months ago. He had made it a chore for her. It was never about her, her satisfaction, her needs. He even told her that if she didn't have sex when he wanted to, he would find another source, because men had needs. Which was complete bullshit. How had she fallen for that?

"He choked you?" The sheriff paused taking notes to look up, sympathy clear in the older man's gray eyes.

"Yes. I tried to make him stop ... but he only laughed and squeezed harder. I scratched his face, and he let go long enough for me to get away. I was in so much pain, and he chased me through the woods. That's when I fell and landed in a stream. I remember the bear..." She closed her eyes. Ribs cracking ... lip busting, eye swelling ... ankle twisting... God, would the pain ever stop?

"Indiana said the bear passed by you and attacked Parker." The sheriff's words interrupted her body reliving the worst moments of her life.

"Uh ... yes, I blacked out. When I woke up, Indiana had brought me here and was trying to clean my wounds." Her hands went to her cheek and brow where Indiana had tended to the injuries with ointment.

"Clive, get the camera from the patrol car. Let's get

some photos." The sheriff stood and nodded at Indiana. "Can I have a word, Mr. Rivers?"

"Sure, Sheriff."

Hadlee waited in the kitchen for the deputy to return, her gaze distant as she kept seeing the bear over and over in her head. The way it had stared at her, the golden-brown eyes deep and its white canine teeth as it roared and surged up the embankment. Chad's earsplitting screams... Then the warm puff of air as the bear returned and huffed and nudged her. Black dots filled her vision. As things had blurred almost beyond recognition, she'd seen something else, hadn't she? Something not quite as big as the bear, but what?

3

Indiana closed the door to his home office, and thankfully Sheriff Wade waited a moment before laying into him.

"What the hell, Indiana? You *killed* a man! You promised me you wouldn't hurt anyone if I let you live here." Wade jerked his hat off his head and smacked it across his thighs as he paced the length of the room. "You promised me that you'd make no trouble. Now I have a dead man up in the hills there, sliced up like Sunday brisket." Wade wiped the back of one hand over his brow as he blew out a breath. "What the hell really happened?"

"Everything I told you over the phone was true. I heard her scream. She was running from that abusive asshole and she fell. He was going to kill her right there in my stream. I saw him kick her hard enough to break her ribs. She can barely breath without pain. She was covered in blood, and he had her pinned down. I think he was going to hold her head underwater with his foot."

"And then?" Wade asked.

"Unofficially?" Indiana asked with a rueful smile.

The sheriff shot him a look that clearly warned now was not the time to be a smartass.

"My bear saw him brutalize a helpless female and when the guy ran ... my bear stopped him."

The sheriff closed his eyes and blew out another breath. "When word gets out, people will come hunting for that bear ... for *you*. Humans don't like a bear that isn't afraid to attack people. It won't be safe here for a shifter, not for a long while. If you stay, you won't be able to change without risking your life."

"I'm aware." Indiana had realized that fact an hour ago, after he gotten off the phone with 911. Bears were killed all the time for straying too close to towns. But a bear that had killed a man deliberately? It would draw every hunter for miles who had something to prove or wanted a trophy for his man cave.

"Christ," Wade muttered. "Who is this woman? Does she know...?"

"No, she passed out before I changed."

"Small miracle," the sheriff muttered. "When the boys are done taking photos, the coroner will load up the body. I need to take that girl into town and have the doc look at her. She might have a few broken ribs, and she ought to have some x-rays done."

"I can drive her," Indiana offered. For some reason he didn't want to let Hadlee out of his sight. It wasn't just his bear who felt overprotective. His bear always been protective of women, but with Hadlee it seemed even more heightened.

"Only if she wants you to. She may want me to drive her instead. The girl's been through hell."

The sheriff had no idea. Indiana's mouth hardened to a grim line. She'd been savagely attacked by a man who she'd put her trust in, a man she'd been romantically involved with. He couldn't imagine a deeper betrayal than a lover trying to kill you.

"I shouldn't say it, not as a law man anyway, but I'm glad that bastard is dead. We don't need people like him still breathing on this planet. Call me old-fashioned, but some crimes don't deserve to go unpunished." The sheriff clapped a hand on Indiana's shoulder. "I'll go ask Ms. Wilson if she wants a ride to town and I'll check on the coroner."

Indiana found Hadlee standing in front of the wall in the kitchen, getting pictures taken of her wounds and self-defense injuries. She looked so small and battered. His bear growled just beneath the surface.

"All done, Ms. Wilson." The deputy put away the camera and turned to nod respectfully at Indiana before he left the room. Hadlee's shoulders sank, and her face was far more pale than it had been a short while ago.

"You need to shower and rest," Indiana said, and put a gentle hand on her shoulder. "Sheriff Wade and I both think you need to visit the medical clinic in town."

"I don't, I'm—"

"Do not say you're fine, honey." Indiana stepped close to her, and she shied away but then relaxed as if she sensed he wouldn't hurt her. That instinct to flinch would take time to fade before she realized she could trust a man again. And he needed an excuse to hold her in his arms, to calm the tempest he could feel brewing in her soul.

"Indiana, please just—"

"No, honey. Sheriff's orders. You can take his car into town, or I can take you. If you go with me, I'll feed you at the best diner in town after the doc's had a good look at you." He wanted to be the one to take her and make sure she was okay, but he wasn't about to force her choices, not after all she'd been through.

"Okay." She glanced out the kitchen window and her lower lip trembled. He glanced in the direction she was looking. The coroner and his assistant were loading up Parker's body which had been retrieved and carried back to the nearest place where the coroner could park his van which was in Indiana's driveway. The corpse was wrapped up in a body bag, but the sight was no less awful.

He'd made that living, breathing human become nothing more than a body, a dead one. It was an awful feeling to be relieved that a murderous creature was dead, but still feel the innate remorse of having taken a life.

Indiana put an arm around Hadlee's shoulder and gently pulled her into his arms, turning her away from the scene. She started to cry, the soft sound of her pain knifing him deep inside places no one had dared touch in years.

"Hush," he murmured as he kept one hand around the back of her head and cradled her against him. "It's over," he promised.

Thump—thump. Her heart beat against his chest in a delicate rhythm for a few minutes before it steadied and matched his own.

What will I do? a voice whispered, and he stilled. That wasn't his voice in his head. It was *hers.* He was hearing her thoughts... He hadn't imagined it? There were only a few reasons a shifter could hear another's thoughts ... and if what he suspected might be true, he was screwed.

You will survive, he thought back, praying she could hear him.

Hadlee turned her head, her green eyes clearing of the pain fog a little and returning back to the dark forest green that made him think of the woods around his home. God, she was lovely. Those eyes held him prisoner. The bruises forming on her skin, the cuts and scrapes, made her look so fragile, so easily hurt. But her eyes? Damn, those eyes held the strength of the mightiest forests, the hardest bedrock, the deepest of the Earth's seas. He knew better than most, that being strong didn't mean one couldn't get hurt. It meant that one survived despite the pain. And this woman? She was stronger than anyone he'd ever met. She was a woman worth killing for, a woman worth protecting against every evil in the world.

"I think I'm ready to go to town."

"All right." He reluctantly released her and went to fetch his keys to the Bronco.

"Well?" the sheriff asked as he met Hadlee and Indiana on the steps outside of Indiana's house.

"I'll be taking her into town," Indiana said.

"That all right with you, Ms. Wilson?" Wade asked.

Hadlee nodded. "I ... um ... I will need some clothes.

My suitcase is in Chad's car in the parking lot south of the trail I told you about. My stuff should still be in the back of the car. He made me leave my phone and keys... He said it would be more romantic to be unplugged during our night beneath the stars." Her voice sounded so hollow as she seemed to realize it had been one more way he'd kept her from reaching help.

"I'll have someone grab it and meet you in town. We have to notify Parker's next of kin after we process his car, which we can do pretty quickly. We can release your luggage to you after that. It shouldn't take more than an hour." The Sheriff gave her a gentle, worried look before he resumed a more business-like expression. "Indy, I'll call you when we can return her possessions to her."

"Thanks, Sheriff." Indiana nodded to him and gently guided Hadlee to his vehicle. He opened the passenger door to the Bronco and lifted her up into the passenger seat. She started to buckle herself in but winced.

"You can leave it off if it causes pain," he said. "I'll drive slow and careful into town."

"I'll be okay," Hadlee replied, and clicked the belt into place.

Indiana followed the sheriff's patrol SUV out of the

woods and onto the dirt road that led to the main street which would take them to town.

Indiana didn't mind the silence; he was good with silence. But he wondered if Hadlee might need conversation as a distraction. She kept wiping at tears as she glanced out the window.

The sight of her tears was fucking killing him. He wanted to roar, to tear down every person who had ever dared to cause those tears. The only solace he had was that he'd ripped out the throat of the man who had done this. God, maybe he should distract her or something... Talk about the weather? No, that was stupid.

Get it together, Indy, he snapped at himself.

"So ... uh ... where are you from?" God, that was just as bad as asking about the weather.

"Chicago, I lived in the suburbs but moved downtown for a job in advertising. That's where I met Chad."

Shit. Was every question he asked going to lead back to that asshole?

"Advertising? What kind?"

"I help create story boards for commercials. I fly to LA a lot to help with the shoots when they're ready to put them on film."

"Really? Do you like that? All the traveling?"

"I did at first, but the novelty of it has worn off. It would be nice to be in one place for a while." She relaxed a little as they talked, and Indiana was glad his distraction strategy worked.

"What about you? Do you just live in the woods here or…?" She looked at him and he realized he had her full attention.

"Me? I've always liked the peace of the woods, ever since I was a child. I can be myself here. I work remotely as a website designer, so it doesn't matter where I live."

"You design websites?" Her eyes widened.

"I don't look like the type, right?" He grinned. He knew he looked more like a lumberjack than a nerd who had an office that looked like some kind of a command center.

"No," she agreed, and laughed softly. The sound was so adorable it punched him in right in the heart.

"You look more like a sexy lumberjack." She stopped giggling and blushed. "Oh my God, I'm sorry, I didn't mean to say that out loud."

Indiana laughed. "I'll take being called a sexy lumberjack any day." Hell, he had been a lumberjack a few years back. Being called sexy was a bonus.

Hadlee grinned. Her blush still flushed her face, but she definitely seemed less embarrassed when she interacted with him.

"I'm surprised a web designer would want to live out here," she added after a moment.

"It's quiet here," he said, his voice soft. "I can think out here. I can *create* out here. My head gets filled with noise in the city, and it's a lot harder to do my job." He couldn't tell her the other part—that as a bear shifter, he needed the woods. If he lived in the city, he would never be able to change, which meant he would repress part of who he was. And that really wasn't living, was it?

"I wouldn't mind the quiet or the woods as long as I felt safe," Hadlee murmured.

"You would," he said. "I'd protect you." Too late he realized what he'd said. "I mean, you'd be safe with anyone you lived next to out here. The residents of Aspen Falls are good people," he said.

"You wouldn't mind having me for your next-door neighbor?" Hadlee asked with a shy smile.

God, she was brave, to want to live in the place where she'd been attacked. Maybe it was because she understood it hadn't been the woods that had been the danger to her, but rather a man.

"I wouldn't mind a neighbor like you," he assured her, and found he was smiling again. His heart gave a wild jolt as she reached over and touched his arm.

"Thank you for finding me. I can't remember if I said that already." Her emerald eyes were large and luminous, and he hated to look away from her to focus on the road.

"You're welcome." His voice was a little gruff as he tried to calm his raging heart. When was the last time he'd felt like this around a woman? Years, certainly.

"How far is town?" She yawned.

"About fifteen minutes. Why don't you get some sleep. I'll wake you when we reach the clinic." He stretched his right arm behind her seat and found his spare blanket. "Use this for a pillow against the window."

"Thanks." She accepted it, folding it up into a makeshift pillow, and was asleep the moment her head hit the blanket.

His bear rumbled in approval at the sight of the little female resting trustingly in his care yet again.

Mine, the bear growled.

Not ours, he argued back. *Can't be ours.*

He couldn't take a human mate. The dangers were too great. Indiana's heart gave a thudding beat as he fought off the sorrow such thoughts brought. Perhaps he would try to visit his father's old clan at the summer solstice. Maybe there would be a female willing to take him as a mate and leave her clan to come here. But that was a long shot. Bear clans were heavily driven by matriarchal support structures. While bears were often solitary creatures, they liked to stay near their clans for support, especially the females. His mother's clan had almost died out; he was the last one. He had nothing to offer a female bear—no clan, no support. Just himself. The only way he'd be welcomed back into a clan was to make his own with a female who had no clan either, or by mating with a female in a preexisting clan. Rogue male bears were not allowed in clans without having mated into them or having been born into them.

He was still thinking things over as they reached the little town of Aspen Falls. It had been his home for the last several years and it was welcoming and warm. He felt safer here than anywhere else he'd lived in a long while. It was as idyllic, with quaint shops and little restaurants and businesses. He didn't spend much of his time in the town, but he'd made friends over the years with many people who lived here.

Indiana stole a glance at the sleeping Hadlee and again his inner bear rumbled in deep satisfaction as he saw she looked less troubled as she slept. The dark smudges under eyes had lessened a little and while her bruises had darkened to a purple shade, she was breathing normally, deeply. He parked the Bronco in front of the medical clinic. Then he reached out and touched her arm. A second later, he regretted the move when she woke up screaming.

4

She shouldn't have screamed. It had been a mistake, but somehow she'd fallen asleep and she'd been dreaming ... of Chad. His hands around her throat, his black eyes so full of hate simply because she was *alive*. She had no strength to fight him in the dream. She'd been even more helpless than she had been when it actually happened.

A soothing, deep baritone voice broke through her spiraling. Her body was still reeling, temporarily locked in the aftermath of the dream. The voice broke through those bad memories, like a hand reaching through the crushing darkness of a vast sea and pulling her back to the surface, where she could breathe.

She stared into the concerned brown eyes that watched her. The man ... Indiana... The man who'd saved her from the bear and carried her to his home. She was safe with...him.

"You okay?" he asked again.

"Yeah, no, it was just a ... bad dream." She brushed her hair out of her face and rubbed her eyes. She felt like she'd been run over by a truck and she knew she would only feel worse tomorrow when the soreness set in. He stared at her a long moment, his gaze gentle but clearly searching for something, but she wasn't sure what. She had the strangest feeling he was going to say something... Something that would profoundly change her life, as mad as it sounded. And she wanted to hear those words that would change her, save her from the maelstrom of pain and fear she'd endured. He blinked suddenly and glanced away, breaking the connection they'd shared in that instant.

"We're ... uh ... at the clinic." Indiana nodded at the building he'd parked in front of. She glanced around little town of Aspen Falls. She had wanted to explore it when she and Chad had driven down Main Street yesterday, but he'd refused. He had been too eager to get to the trail and now she knew why. Her stomach turned queasy again and her chest tightened. Shoving thoughts of Chad away, she studied the little shops with their cheery storefronts. It was exactly the way she pictured a cozy small town should look, and she loved it.

"This is Aspen Falls? It's beautiful. I wanted to stop here and … never got the chance." She managed to give him a brief smile, which felt totally worth her aching face.

"Wait a second. I'll help you out." He watched her for a moment before he got out of the car and walked around to her side to open the door for her.

Then he lifted her up and set her down with such gentleness and ease she felt like a little kitten in his large hands. He went up the steps to the clinic door ahead of her and opened it, letting her pass in front of him to enter. A bell jingled above their heads and Hadlee recoiled from the sudden, unexpected sound.

"Easy," Indiana whispered, and put a hand on her lower back, letting her feel his presence behind her.

A single receptionist at a desk behind a sliding glass window and looked up as they approached. The woman's smile faltered into a shocked look as she saw Hadlee.

"The sheriff mentioned you'd be coming in." The woman pulled out a clipboard. "You feel okay enough to fill this out for me? We'll get you back to the doc soon and she'll get you all sorted out."

"Yes, thanks." Hadlee hesitantly collected the clipboard and eased into a chair in the waiting room to fill out the intake form. Her hand ached, but she scribbled her information down as quickly as she could. She had a feeling it would be hard to be around new people for a while, even nice ones. Only Indiana seemed to make her feel comfortable.

Hadlee returned the clipboard when she was done and promised to call the clinic with her insurance information once the police were done with her suitcase and backpack. She was taken back to an exam room by a male nurse who took her vitals and told her the doctor would be in to see her soon. As she'd been taken back, she'd glanced at Indiana, afraid he'd leave.

"I'll be right outside," he promised. "I won't leave."

How did he know what she needed to hear? Why did she need so much to hear him, a complete stranger, say that to her?

She sat on the edge of the exam table, flinching at the crinkling paper beneath her.

She hadn't been waiting long at all before the exam room door was opened by a woman in a long doctor's coat with honey colored hair pulled into a ponytail. Her eyes were blue and full of a deep kindness that couldn't be faked.

"Hadlee Wilson?" she asked, glancing over the chart she picked up from the end of the table.

"Yes."

"Sheriff Wade called in and told me to expect you. I'm Doctor Ember Ravenwood." The woman flipped through the chart as she spoke.

"Nice to meet you." Hadlee tried for a smile but felt the wobble at the edges of her lips.

"Uh-uh," Dr. Ravenwood shook her head in a kind way. "You don't have to do that, not here."

"Do what?"

"Pretend you're okay." Dr. Ravenwood stepped closer and Hadlee realized with a start that the woman was around her own age, maybe slightly older, and stunningly beautiful.

"You know it's *okay* to not be okay. Now, walk me through things. Tell me what happened but focus on what that assho—er ... assailant did to you physically. I need to list the injuries in my report for the sheriff's office, but also I need to know what to treat you for."

Hadlee drew in a deep breath and explained the story again. God, when would all of this be over? She just wanted to go home to Chicago. But even home didn't feel as safe as Indiana's cabin.

When she was done, Dr. Ravenwood x-rayed her ankle, confirmed it was just a sprain, and gave her a special soft ice pack that fit around her foot. The rest of her injuries were patched up and her broken ribs examined with care after yet another x-ray. The doctor explained that the fractures were small, and she would heal well. Hadlee's orders were clear: She was to rest and to stay in town for a few weeks if her job would allow it, so she could avoid the strain of a long drive or flight back to Chicago.

Hadlee called her boss before leaving the exam room, briefly explained the situation, and they allowed her another week of time off. She'd already requested a full week for her intended trip with Chad so all she really had to do was get approved for a second week. The nurse filled a prescription of antibiotics and pain meds, and she was sent back into the small waiting room.

Indiana's large, muscled frame was squeezed into one of the tiny little chairs. He had a children's magazine open sideways, and seemed to be studying some sort of maze on the page. He growled and put the magazine back down, scowling. She giggled and the sound had him bolting out of his chair to face her.

"You ready to go home?"

Home. His home. For a moment she almost thought it was hers too.

"Yes, I have medicine and my instructions for my ankle and my ribs." She waved the bag containing her medications and the icepack.

"Good." He took the bag from her and led her outside to the car. Her stomach rumbled when they were halfway there.

"Wait, you mentioned something about taking me to the best diner in town?" she asked. He had offered to get her food, hadn't he? Normally she wouldn't have reminded someone of an offer, but she was starving.

Indiana's concerned frown vanished. "I did, didn't I?" He grinned and pointed to a business across the street. "It's right there."

A hand-painted sign that said *Jo's Joint* hung above the windows of a restaurant.

Indiana walked with her across the street, and they chose a booth by the big window once they were inside. A woman in her late forties who wore a light-blue dress with an apron came over to take their order. Her dark hair was lightly threaded with silver and pulled into a messy but somehow completely elegant-looking bun, with loose tendrils which framed her face. Her gray eyes were sharp enough to miss nothing, but they held no judgment.

"Afternoon, Indy." The woman smiled at him and pulled her notepad out of her apron pocket. "The usual? Full pancake stack, two eggs, sausage, and a bowl of oatmeal?"

"That'd be great, thanks," Indiana said. "Jo, this is Hadlee, she—"

Jo's face softened and she placed a hand on Hadlee's shoulder. "What do you want, sweetheart? Whatever it is, it's on the house. We serve breakfast all day, plus lunch and dinner."

"Oh, but I can pay you—" Hadlee began.

"Honey, we women stick together. Now let me feed you. What would you like?"

A little flustered, Hadlee examined the diner's laminated menu. "Um … could I have French toast please? And hot chocolate?"

"Done." Jo walked back toward the kitchen to drop the order off.

"Why do I get the feeling she knows what happened to me?" Hadlee whispered to Indiana. She was completely mortified, but another part of her was deeply touched by the woman's care and concern.

"That's the hazard of being in a small town. Everyone knows your business all the time." The way he scowled as he said this gave Hadlee the feeling he wasn't just talking about her business. "The people in this town are good. Hell, most small towns in the middle of the country are. They remember what it means to be a community. You look out for everyone." Indiana glanced out the window, his face shadowed with unspoken words, which Hadlee saw quite clearly were full of pain.

"Have you always lived here?" she asked a little hesitantly. She didn't want to overtly pry into her rescuer's life, but she did want to understand him.

"No, not here. I was born in Indiana."

She flashed him a disbelieving look.

He blushed. "It's true—and yeah, that's where the name comes from. My parents were natural roamers, and my mom thought it would be a nice reminder of where I was born. I guess it's good she settled on the name of the state, rather than the town, given I was born in a place called Boonville."

Hadlee surprised herself with a laugh. "Boonville? That would have made for a fun name."

He rolled his eyes but grinned.

She sobered and tilted her head at him. "You said your parents were natural roamers—does that mean you didn't stay in Indiana long?"

He nodded. "After Indiana, we headed west, I think. I don't remember a lot of the details before we ended up in Alaska."

The slight hitch in his tone pinged some instinct in

the back of Hadlee's brain, but she pressed on. "How old were you in Alaska?"

"When I left I was about fourteen." He blew out a breath and rubbed a hand down his face. "My parents died there, in a car accident. And then it was just me, on my own."

"Wait—at fourteen? What about Child Protective Services? Hadlee leaned towards him, concerned to know how a fourteen-year-old boy had grown into a man all alone.

He shook his head. "My community was really small. Child Protective Services wasn't really aware of us. There wasn't anyone I could stay with, so I left. I made my way south through Canada and then into the states. I passed some time in Montana before heading to Washington. I worked a lot of odd jobs, first logging and then other types of manual labor. Then I started showing my bosses my natural computer skills. I studied for my GED at night and after I passed, I applied for college in Colorado and got in with a full ride thanks to my test scores. I studied computer engineering, graphic design, and coding. After getting my degrees, I moved here, bought my land, and built my house."

Hadlee gazed at him in complete awe. He had taken control of his life and made it exactly what he wanted, no matter the obstacles. God, she envied him. When he caught her staring, she blushed and looked down at the table between them.

"You're lucky," she whispered. "When my parents died, I thought I could handle everything. My life seemed like I was always one mistake away from a complete disaster. Somehow I managed to keep my head above water, finish college, and get a job, but I haven't felt like I've been going in the right direction for some time." She twirled her napkin between her fingertips. "How did you know where you wanted life to lead you?"

Indiana's jaw clenched briefly, and then he relaxed and sipped his coffee.

"I suppose the simplest answer is that I searched for peace," he said after a long moment. "Wherever I felt my instincts pulling me, that's where I headed, and they brought me here. I haven't moved in seven years. For me, that's a long time. It's the closest I've ever felt to true peace."

She rubbed her arms, suppressing a shiver. "I feel it too, that sense of calm here. It was strange, but when Chad and I started our hike, I had the oddest feeling, like I was supposed to be here. I guess that's one of the reasons why I never expected him to do ... what he did."

Indiana reached across the table and clasped one of her hands in his own.

"Use the words, Hadlee. Say them and they will hold less power over you."

"He attacked me." She exhaled and Indiana gave her an encouraging nod. "Is it weird that it felt like the woods protected me? When Chad tried to kill me, it was like the trees were listening? Maybe that bear heard me, or the trees or... Hell, I don't know what I'm saying. I sound crazy, don't I?" she asked. Butterflies stormed against the walls of her belly as he curled his fingers tighter around her own and held her gaze.

"That's not crazy," Indiana replied. "Nature has its own laws, which sometimes are more brutal but ultimately more fair than men would allow."

"Well, if the trees were listening, I'm grateful to them."

When Jo returned with their orders, Hadlee was stunned by how hungry she was. Indiana didn't seem to notice she ate everything on her plate. Chad always made snide comments about her weight. She stilled with the last bite of her food perched on her fork. God, when had she become such a fool? He'd been controlling her through food too, basically starving her because he was an abusive, narcissistic asshole.

She ate the last bite of her French toast, truly

savoring the taste and knowing she was free of him. She was done with Chad; done with all the brainwashing he had subjected her to in only six months.

She wanted her life back.

INDIANA FELT SOMETHING CHANGE IN THE LITTLE FEMALE IN front of him. The whisper of her thoughts teased his mind like murmurs on the other side of a gossamer curtain. Sometimes he could hear her almost as clearly as he could hear his own thoughts and the thoughts of his bear. Other times her inner voice was completely silent or very muted. What did it mean? He had always believed it was a sign of a true mate to hear the other person's thoughts, but he'd begun to believe what little he'd been told about mates might be nothing more than a fairy tale.

Was mating with a human and having a true mate connection with one even possible? Not having grown up in a bear clan, he knew far less about his own species than other bears did. He hadn't been lying to Hadlee when he'd said his community was small. And by the time he'd visited a bear clan in Montana, he'd been too embarrassingly old to ask questions like this of the other bear shifters. He still had the contact information for the alpha of that clan though. Perhaps he should call him and ask some questions when he had a chance. The alpha had become a friend to him and while he hadn't called him often, he knew his friend would answer if he did.

"Thank you for breakfast. I can't believe how hungry I was." Hadlee pushed her empty plate away and let out a sigh of pure satisfaction. As a bear who loved to eat, he knew the sound well and it aroused him to hear it from a female. If she stayed with him for a while, he would cook for her and make sure she had plenty to eat. A well-fed female was a happy female. He'd been raised to believe females should be happy, and it was his job as a male to make his female happy.

She wasn't his though, damnit. No matter how much he might want her to be.

He cleared his throat before replying. "You're welcome." When his cell phone vibrated in his pocket, he pulled it out and glanced at the text. "The sheriff says your suitcase and other belongings are ready to be released to you. We can pick them up now if you want."

She brightened. "That would be great, if it's not too much trouble."

"It's not," he promised. He liked being around this

woman, liked her smile, her laugh, the way she talked and her thoughts about the world. He'd only just begun to get to know her, and he was already completely fascinated.

He left a few bills on the table to pay for their breakfast and waved at Jo before they left.

"You bring her back soon, Indy," Jo called after them.

"She's really nice," Hadlee commented as she stepped out onto the street. "She reminds me of a protective mama bear."

This comparison made him laugh. "She would make a good mother bear."

He escorted Hadlee to the sheriff's station at the far end of the main street and once inside, they met the receptionist, Tiffany.

"Hey Indy, heard you got babysitting duty." Tiffany was close to Hadlee's age, and she shot Hadlee a sympathetic look. "I heard what happened, Miss Wilson. I am glad you're okay."

"Thanks," Hadlee said.

Indiana was glad Tiffany was supporting Hadlee, not judging her. Too often he'd seen people blame the victim of an assault and it was time that changed.

"Sheriff!" Tiffany called over her shoulder toward the open office door behind her. The glass walls revealed the sheriff seated at his desk with a slew of case files stacked haphazardly around him. He glanced up and waved at Indiana and Hadley. Then he hit an intercom button on his desk and spoke to someone before he came out to meet them.

The sheriff cleared throat. "Ms. Wilson, we contacted Mr. Parker's family, and they have been informed of his death. I wanted to speak with you about how much you want me to tell them concerning what happened before he was killed."

"You mean the assault?" Hadlee asked.

She started to tremble, and Indiana put a hand on her shoulder. She seemed to calm a little at his touch, and he lightly squeezed his fingers, massaging the tension out of her muscles.

"Yes. Given that he's dead, we can't exactly press charges for the assault. There's no way for us to prose-cute him for the crimes against you. But we can still share the details of what happened. It's your choice."

Hadlee glanced down at the floor, then suddenly turned to face Indiana. "What would you do?"

He was stunned that she wanted to know what he would do, but it also humbled him that she would trust him and his opinions.

"If it was me, I would tell everything. But that means people will look at you and know what happened to you. The assault doesn't change who you are, no matter how differently everyone might look at you. You are the one who must decide what matters to you. The truth can hurt, but sometimes it is the right choice."

She bit her bottom lip, her green eyes large and luminous as she stared back at him. He could feel the flutter of her thoughts in his head.

Can't let anyone know … but it isn't right for people to mourn the death of a monster, were her unspoken words.

Hadlee faced the sheriff again. "I want to tell the truth about everything."

Wade shot a look at Indiana, and Indiana knew what the man was thinking.

Not everything. No one could know a bear shifter had killed Chad Parker.

"Very well. I will inform the authorities in Chicago and Parker's family." Wade retrieved some paperwork from Tiffany's desk. "Sign these release forms for your belongings."

Hadlee signed the papers and handed them back to Wade.

"Could you stay in town a few days more, just in case we need to conduct any follow-up interviews or have questions? There's a nice little motel about midway down Main Street."

"Or you can stay with me," Indiana volunteered at once, shocking himself. "If you want to, that is," he adding in a slightly embarrassed murmur as he stared into the forest of her eyes. She wouldn't want to stay with him, a stranger, a man, the damned bear who'd killed her boyfriend. What was he even thinking?

"Um … that might be good, if you don't mind," she said after a moment.

"Are you sure, Ms. Wilson?" Wade asked. "You would be out in the woods where that bear attacked you."

Indiana shot the sheriff a hard glare.

"Honestly, the woods don't scare me, sheriff. The bear attacked Chad and left me alone. Besides, I think I rather like the quiet out there."

Wade sighed. "Well, it's quiet in town most of the time too."

Indiana snorted. "Only during the day. At night, loggers, farmers, and cowboys come to town to hit the bar and grill for drinks and dancing. It's not so quiet then."

"True enough," Wade agreed. "Well, let's get your stuff, Ms. Wilson." Wade went into the evidence lockup room and brought back a rolling suitcase and a backpack.

"We put your wallet and phone inside your hiker gear bag," the sheriff said.

Indiana took the backpack before Hadlee could grasp it and slung it over his shoulder. Then he collected the rolling suitcase in his other hand.

"Indiana, you don't have to—"

"You're still healing," he reminded her. "I don't think the doc would like you tossing suitcases around with those broken ribs."

She finally sighed, acquiescing. "Thanks, Sheriff," she said.

"Sure thing." Wade nodded back at her.

Tiffany called out as they reached the door. "If you want to hang with any girls, Hadlee, you call the station for my cell phone number. Jo and I like to go tease the cowboys on weekends, and tomorrow night is Saturday night."

"Thanks," Hadlee said to Tiffany, her face flushed red with a blush.

Indiana grunted as he exited the station. There was no way he'd let Hadlee tease any cowboys. The bear in him agreed. It was too dangerous to let her be around men after she'd been hurt. She needed to be rested, fed, and ... well, cuddled, damnit. And that was what bears did best. As soon as he could, he wanted to get her bundled up on his lap and just hold her until her fears subsided. But he'd have to work to earn her trust.

He loaded Hadlee's luggage in the back of the Bronco and helped her into the vehicle.

"You still want to stay with me?" he asked one more time.

Her face was still red as she nodded. "You feel safe. I probably have some kind of rescuer syndrome, but it's true. The woods feel safe too. Even the bear—" She halted.

"Even the bear what?" he asked, bracing one booted foot on the runner of the Bronco as he kept the passenger door open to talk to her.

She fiddled with her seatbelt straps. "Even the bear feels safe. The worst he could do was kill me and maybe eat me, but then I'd be dead. So it wouldn't matter."

He hated this, hated that women had to frame the world in such a way that being dead was safer than having to suffer unspeakable horrors at the hands of men. Half the population of this planet lived nearly every day of their lives in terror and fear of what the other half would do to them. He couldn't imagine what that would be like.

"I know good men exist. I know not *all* men are like Chad, but we don't have a way to tell the good from the bad," Hadlee admitted, as if reading Indiana's thoughts.

Indiana reached up, cupping her chin in his palm. She was so touchable. He felt like a villain for thinking about how much he wanted to hold her and do so much more, especially after what she'd been through. He started to pull his hand away, but she leaned forward, catching his wrist with her slender, beautiful fingers.

"You keep pulling away from me like that, why?" she asked.

"I figured the last thing you want is a man touching you."

"Oh, right..." Her shoulders sagged slightly. "But Chad was the one who hurt me. Indy, you aren't Chad. I don't want to be forced to give up physical contact with people, especially men, just because of him."

God, this woman was brave. He wouldn't blame her if she wanted nothing to do with men in general ever again, but here she was, stating she refused to let that asshole ruin her life, even after he was dead.

"Okay," he said after a moment. "But if I do or say anything you don't like, you need to tell me. I don't know what it is about you but..." *But I want to touch you,* he added silently.

Then touch me, her voice replied in his head, startling him. He blinked. The thought had been so clear, like when he'd heard her pleas for help in the woods.

He once more lifted his hand to cup her chin and

stopped letting his doubts crowd his mind. Indiana brushed the pad of his thumb over her bottom lip, lost in thoughts of taking that lip between his teeth and nibbling away at it. Bears did like to nibble. A lot. And Hadlee was as edible as they came. Just thinking that she might be a mate for him was too dangerous, too tempting. His bear was going to be impossible to control for long.

"Let's get you back to my place so you can shower and rest."

While she did, he would have a few calls to make in order to get some answers about what he and his bear were feeling for her.

5

Hadlee stared at the big shower in the guest suite of Indiana's home. Was it possible to be intimidated by a beautiful bathroom? Indiana stood beside her, dominating the room despite the vastness of the stunning space. She nearly leaned into the heat that came off his body. He seemed so warm, so strong and stable, whereas she felt so cold and frail. It was as though one stiff wind could blow her away.

"Shampoo, conditioner, soap, and shower gel are inside the shower niche." Indiana opened the shower door and Hadlee spotted the amber-colored bottles of beauty and hair care products sitting on shelves within the tiled walls. She glanced at him. He was well shaven and smelled good, but he definitely hadn't come across as a man who knew his way around nice personal products.

"Spare toothbrushes, razors, and deodorant are in the drawers." He gestured to the gray painted cabinets beneath the white granite countertops.

"Wow ... do you have a lot of visitors?" she asked, trying not to sound overly curious.

A wry smile curved his lips as he gazed down at her. "Not as much as I would like. Even though I like to be alone out here, there are times when I wish these rooms had friends or family in them. Hell, I'd love to have a couple of cubs someday."

"Cubs?"

He rubbed the back of his neck and glanced away. "I mean kids. You know, sometimes I jokingly call them cubs, like little bear cubs." His eyes lit with a ginger-colored fire that made his entire face seem to glow with joy at the thought, despite his obvious embarrassment of talking about something that seemed so intimate.

"Oh, right, like Boy Scouts call the little ones Cub Scouts?" she asked.

"Yeah, something like that." He cleared his throat. "Take your time in the shower. I'll have dinner ready later tonight. Until then, all you need to do is shower and sleep."

Shower and sleep. Those words sounded like pure

heaven. Hadlee was relieved at receiving his gentle orders. She still felt so scattered emotionally and physically. Having some direction given to her helped her focus on what she needed to do.

"Thank you, Indy."

He turned back to face her and cupped her chin in his hand as he looked at her.

"Honey, you have to stop thanking me. There are still good people out there. You are safe and you deserve to be safe. A woman should never have to thank a man for his protection or help. Being safe is a right you should demand, not one gifted by men who will barter for things from you."

She knew he was right, but they both understood that for far too long, society had let men set the rules, rules that had forced women to turn over their bodies, their freedom, even their lives to men, on the promise of safety with the irony that most women who were victims of assault were attacked by their own domestic partners.

Just like she had been...

Still studying her closely, he stroked his thumb over her bottom lip. "If you need me, I'll be in the den," Indiana said.

"The den?" she asked.

"Yeah, the big room with the leather sectional and TV."

"Oh, right." Hadlee nodded. He meant family room. She forgot that some people called that room a den. Den was such a cozy word, and she really liked it.

He gave her one more assessing gaze before he dropped his hand from her face and stepped back. He left her and closed the door to give her privacy. She waited a minute before undressing and turning on the shower. The process of removing her clothes was painful and she ended up slowly peeling off each item. Her body protested each movement, her ribs aching and her muscles twinging. She adjusted the water temperature of the shower.

A waterfall spray above her and angled nozzles on the sides of the shower created an all-encompassing feeling of water hitting her skin from everywhere. She adjusted the temperature, making it hotter, as her skin felt cold and clammy. Hadlee winced as the spray hit her cuts and scrapes. She knew Indiana had supplies and she could redress her wounds later. She moved slowly, feeling a heavy stiffness settle in her limbs from being injured. She was *really* going to hurt tomorrow.

Tomorrow. She used to look forward to the future, to what each new day could bring, but she no longer did that. The past held pain, and the future seemed bleak. All she could hold onto was the present. But even that was almost impossible without creating panic attacks.

Chad was dead. She would have to face his parents, maybe even his friends and coworkers. What about her job? Her boss, her friends and coworkers? Everything was going to get worse before it got better, assuming it would ever get better. Her chest suddenly collapsed, and she couldn't breathe. She sucked in a strangled breath and again her chest nearly caved in as her lungs ceased to work.

Can't breathe ... can't think... She slumped into a ball on the floor in the shower, curling on her side, fighting for breath. The door to the bathroom slammed open and she jerked, lifting her head up enough to stare up at the hulking figure of a man on the other side of the expensive fogged glass.

"Fuck, Hadlee, I'm sorry but I'm coming in," Indiana warned in a low growl.

She was shivering, despite the warmth of the water and didn't move as he opened the shower door. He kicked off his boots and pulled off his socks, but he still wore his jeans and a dark-green T-shirt.

"You—you'll ruin ... your clothes," she said through chattering teeth.

"Shit, my clothes don't matter," he muttered as he

stepped into the shower. He eased his large frame down beside her. Then he reached over and lifted her up, pulling her onto his lap so he could cradle her. His strong arms banded around her. He rested his chin on top of her head and enveloped her within a manly cocoon. Somewhere in the back of her mind she registered she was naked on his lap, but it didn't matter compared to the agony of her lungs and brain screaming for oxygen.

"*Breathe* for me," he whispered in a low, slightly rough voice. Something about his tenderness broke the cement wall that had encased her lungs, and she started to sob, which let in heaving lungfuls of air.

Little by little she breathed deeper, and the shivers began to fade. She inhaled his scent. He smelled like the trees, earth, and fresh rain. Her mind moved away from thoughts of death and pain and focused on the scent of rain. How could he smell so wonderful?

Petrichor... That was the word he made her think of. It was the bacteria in the soil that blossomed after rain. Only humans could smell it—a trait humans had developed over thousands of years of evolution. Where humans smelled Petrichor, there was fertile soil to plant crops and water to drink.

Her mind drifted, suddenly picturing raindrops

falling in slow motion all around her to land upon leaves and earth. She saw moss and mushrooms blossom. She glimpsed rabbits and deer licking the rain off leaves and blades of grass. Rainbow glints of trout in the cold, crystalline waters of the stream and the dark shiny surfaces of river stones... The rumble of a distant storm moved through her bones, and she felt the wind move through her thick fur...

Fur?

Hadlee blinked and she was back in the shower. Naked in Indiana's lap.

Oh my God... She tried to move but he held onto her tightly.

"Easy, honey," he said. "Easy, you're still coming down from that rush of emotions. Just—"

"Let me go!" she demanded, her voice pitched to a frantic level.

He released her immediately and she scrambled off his lap and stood, trying to cover herself with her hands and failing.

"Good, you're breathing again," he said as he got to his feet. He kept his gaze averted from her. "Now that you're okay, I'll go."

"Wait!" she blurted out without thinking. He halted, his hand on the shower door. "Just wait," she said again. She didn't want him to leave. But what did she want?

The smell of him was making her a bit dizzy but not in a bad way. That smell of rain and something more ... human filled the space within her, creating a molten heat inside her body that had nothing to do with the hot water. Indiana's T-shirt was molded to his muscled frame, and she was so very aware of how strong he was. His body was corded steel, and even the area round his groin featured a hard bulge pressing against his jeans. He was turned on ... by her? Rather than terrify her, the fact filled her with a shivery excitement she hadn't felt in so long. She tried to focus herself back on the conversation she was supposed to be having with him.

"Sorry. I'm just a little freaked out. But I..." She bit her lip. "I want you to stay. I want to forget him. I want to feel something again and make sure I'm not broken."

At her embarrassing confession he turned around, his eyes staying on her face rather than dropping to her naked body. Why didn't he make a move?

"Tell me exactly what you want, Hadlee. That's how this has to work. When it comes to sex, you call the shots on everything we do."

Hadlee licked her lips. "Kiss me?" It came out a question.

"You sure?" He frowned as he slowly backed her into the walled corner of the large shower. His gaze strayed from her eyes, finally dropping down to her lips. She saw primal hunger in his face that gave her delicious shivers.

"Yeah, I'm sure," she whispered. "But you need to do it. I've never been the one to make the first move with a guy."

"I can do that." He stepped even closer, cornering her fully against the wall as he reached up to cup her chin and tilt her head back so he could gaze down at her. "Tell me to stop at any time," Indiana said before he lowered his head and kissed her.

His lips were soft, warm, and so perfect as he moved his mouth over hers. She parted her lips, flicking her tongue against his, and he growled in encouragement. Then he deepened the kiss, pressing her tighter to the shower wall, her bare breasts rubbing against his wet shirt. Above them the hot water rained down like they were caught in a tropical storm with heat and steam curling around their bodies.

He tasted *good*. She'd almost forgotten that a kiss could be pure magic, that it could set her soul flying. She clutched his shoulders and lifted one leg, curling it around his hip to get even closer. Her pelvis rubbed against his jean-clad thigh. The slightly rough texture of the denim excited her clit as she pressed against him. Zings of pleasure went through her so unexpectedly that she gasped against his lips. He suddenly braced his hands on the tile on either side of her head and continued to kiss her as he moved his hips in a slow roll into her body, letting her ride his thigh the way she so desperately needed.

"That's it, honey, you take what you need," he murmured before kissing down to her neck and then his teeth grazed her shoulder.

Heat exploded through her as he lightly bit down, like some animal holding his mate still. Just the idea made her climax so suddenly and so hard she screamed. The raw, throaty sound echoed throughout the bathroom and beneath it was a rumbling, pleased sound coming from Indiana. She'd never heard a man make a sound like that, so primal, so animalistic. The sound conjured up images of being bent over and fucked hard, of her taking him deep, hard and fast and not being able to walk afterward without feeling him between her thighs. She shook hard, her legs shuddering as her body reacted to the mental image as powerfully as it had to the climax she'd just experienced.

Panting, she clung to him, moving her hips in wild, desperate circles over and over against his leg as she rode out the aftershocks of the climax. It felt so good, this wave of pleasure that continued to roll through her like the tide coming in over and over.

It had been four months since she'd felt this way. Four months since she'd felt anything but a duty to satisfy someone else's needs. For the first time in forever, she remembered she had desires, she had needs, and that a man could fulfill them.

Indiana's warm breath on her neck felt good. Something wet dragged along her shoulder. His tongue? Why was it weirdly hot that he was licking the sore spot between her neck and shoulder? Her body clenched again, and she let out a little moan as he kissed his way back up to her lips.

"You okay?" he asked as he finally pulled his head back to look at her.

"Uh-huh." She nodded, feeling slightly dazed.

Water droplets caught on the tips of his long dark lashes, and she stared at his eyes, utterly fascinated. His hands held onto her gently, and she could still feel that undeniable electric charge between them. What they'd just done had only briefly tempered the need for *more*.

Please kiss me again, she thought with a quiet, desperate longing that tore into her very soul.

His gaze seemed to flare with an almost silvery shimmering light as he swallowed hard and gave his head the minutest of shakes. He spoke in a hoarse but determined tone.

"Let's get you cleaned up." He had to reach around her to pump shampoo into his hands and she turned, offering her back to him. He moved closer behind her, a soft growl escaping his lips. Was he angry with her? She peeped at him over her shoulder, but she saw the farthest thing from anger one could see in another's eyes. Yet she dared not give it a name.

He gently shampooed her hair and rubbed body wash over her. She let him touch her everywhere and he cared for her bruised limbs and scraped skin as if she were a fragile little bird that had been battered in a storm. He didn't try to use her, he simply *cared* for her.

After he turned off the water, he dried her in a large, fluffy, white towel. Then without a word, he scooped her up into his arms and carried her into a bedroom. But it wasn't the guest bedroom. Was it his room? The large sleigh bed had a blue, gray, and green flannel duvet cover accented with silvery gray pillows. He pulled back the covers and nestled her, still wrapped up in the towel, under the blankets.

There was no way she could sleep like this. She felt like a human burrito.

"Indy..." His name came out in a yawn.

"Yeah honey?"

"I don't..." She paused, snuggled deeper into the bed. His scent, strong but welcoming, was all over the pillow.

"Never mind," she whispered and fell blissfully into the gray world of sleep.

Indiana watched her slip into a deep and untroubled sleep. Earlier she'd slept with a furrowed brow as she'd curled up in the Adirondack chair on the back balcony, but now her face was smooth and her expression serene. He leaned against the door jamb, watching her for a long minute before his wet clothes started to bother him. He closed his bedroom door and stepped into the master bathroom. Thankfully her scent wasn't in this room.

Her sweet natural perfume and that honeyed arousal filling the air had made his skin tingle with the need to let his bear free. She had brought out the animal in him. For the first time ever, his bear wanted a female, but she was human. Even if he could have her in his life, he could only share his human side with her, not his wild one. His bear grumbled and huffed in protest, but Indiana knew he was right. What if he showed her his ability to shift and she freaked out, or worse, went to the authorities and told them what he was? He couldn't reveal the existence of shifters to humans. It would put so many innocent lives in danger.

Indiana showered quickly, wrapped a towel around his waist, and passed back through his bedroom where Hadlee was still sleeping soundly. Then he headed out to the kitchen, put Jones's dinner in a bowl, and set it on the floor for the dog before he retrieved his cell phone from the counter. It took Indiana only a moment to find the number he had saved in his contacts. He hit call and held his breath.

"Dane here," came a clipped, rough voice.

"Dane, it's Indiana."

"No shit." The other man chuckled. "Been wondering where you ended up, cub."

Indiana smiled at the affectionate way the other man called him cub. He had been young when he'd passed through Dane's clan. He'd been barely seventeen.

"I'm in Colorado. Little place called Aspen Falls. How is your clan?"

"Oh, you know, same as usual. We're having a mating moon in a few months and you're welcome to come see if any of the females might be a suitable mate for you."

"About that…" Indiana drew in a breath. "I have a question for you. Hell, make it a dozen questions."

"Oh? About one of our females?"

"No, about mating. You know that my mother and father were the last of their clan. I never knew much about the rituals of mating, or anything about true mates beyond the childhood tales my mother told me. They died before we could really talk about that. Could you … could you tell me?"

Dane laughed, but it was a warm sound. "What, you want the birds and the bees talk? Or should I say the birds and the *bears*?"

"Fuck," Indiana grumbled. "This was a mistake. You don't have to tell me anything." He was about ready to hang up. He already felt like a fool having to ask about mating at his age, but he needed answers.

Dane stifled a chuckle. "Wait. I'll tell you everything I know. Shifter matings are unpredictable. Most of the time you have a mate who is the same species as you. But there have been a decent number of times where a bear has formed an irresistible mate connection with another kind. One of our males ended up with a mountain lion. One of our females chose a tiger."

Indiana's heart sank a little. "So no one has mated

to a human then? My mother said it could happen, but she never went into any details." He tried to hide the disappointment in his tone.

"Humans? Sure, of course. The difficulty with mating with a human is that the human must fully seal their bond to you. That's the only way they will be allowed to shift into the same animal as you. There's also the loyalty issue. If a human doesn't fully bond to you, they can still desire other people, whereas once a shifter claims their true mate, they crave and desire only that mate."

Humans could shift if they fully bonded to their mate? His mother had never mentioned such a thing was possible. The realization of what *could be* filled his heart with a leap of joy, but he forced himself to check his emotions.

"A human can really shift? I didn't know that was possible." That more than anything gave Indiana a surge of hope. If he was lucky enough to find his mate and claim her, and she bonded to him, they could shift together, and his bear wouldn't be alone.

"It's rare. Humans have less ability to be certain of their affections enough to bond. They aren't used to the idea of true mates."

"Oh." Indiana sighed and leaned against the marble island.

"Does this mean you found a human mate?" Dane asked, his voice softening with understanding.

"Maybe. What are the signs of a true mate?"

"Well," the other bear shifter began. "They will pull you toward them like a magnet with their sheer presence. You'll feel protective and possessive. You might even sense or hear their thoughts. Once you're fully bonded, your thoughts and hers will be open to one another. You can learn to shield, of course, for privacy when you need it, but there will be a natural openness between you. Most mates don't learn how to censor their thoughts until after a completed claiming."

Indiana stared out the windows at the woods, thinking. "Is it possible to hear a human's thoughts and not be a true mate to them?" he asked.

Dane was quiet a long moment. "No, I don't believe that's possible. If you are hearing a female's thoughts and you're certain that it's *her* thoughts and not another nearby shifter, she's a possible true mate to you. Fate and destiny can give us more than one possible mate, but if I were you, if you are hearing her thoughts, whoever she is, she's your destiny."

My destiny. My mate.

"Thank you, Dane."

"I suggest you claim her now, Indy. Don't wait. Humans are notoriously fragile. Their lives end so swiftly and so easily," Dane warned. "Mates make us whole. Don't miss your chance."

Indiana thanked him again and hung up. Jones finished his dinner and whined for a treat from his Milk-Bone jar. Indiana fed the dog one of his bones and Jones wagged his tail enthusiastically as he scarfed it down. Indiana scratched Jones behind the ears as he took in everything Dane had just told him.

His mate would be asleep for a long while. It was time to shift to and let his bear have a few minutes outside again, since it might be a some time before he could shift without fear of hunters coming after him.

Indiana dropped the bath towel and walked out of his front door and down the steps. A moment later, his body twisted and reshaped into the bear. He dug his claws into the earth and then scented the wind. The wildness called to him, whispering the secrets of the trees and the ancient dreams of the ferns that formed the underbrush in the woods ahead of him.

Nature's language had a thousand beautiful dialects, and he was fluent in every one, from the cry of the fox to the babble of water over river stones. It was easy not to feel lonely if he let himself feel and hear the world around him moving, living, and breathing. Yes, one was never alone when one remembered they were a part of this wild, wonderful world. But it would be something else to share this feeling with another of his kind ... his *mate*. Could he have that with Hadlee? She would have to trust him and trust herself. But she was damned brave. If anyone could do it, he believed she could.

All he had to do was let her discover the wild within herself.

6

Hadlee cuddled deeper in the bed, her body rubbing against a soft towel. *A towel?* What was she doing with a towel in bed? She blinked against the muted light and moved cautiously in the king-size bed. This wasn't Indiana's guestroom. It was *his* bedroom. *Oh God...*

Her memory caught up with her and she relived the erotic encounter with Indiana in the shower, sending fresh waves of warmth through her cold limbs. She'd basically humped him like a horny teenager and came harder than she had in *years*.

It should have been something to celebrate, or be embarrassed by, but the strongest emotion that caught her tight in its hold was guilt. She'd practically had sex with a stranger less than a day after her boyfriend was killed.

What the hell is wrong with me?

Hadlee sat up and grimaced as she realized she was naked beneath the bath towel. When she glanced around the room, she discovered Indiana had moved her suitcase from the guestroom to this room. It sat against the wall by the door. Keeping her towel wrapped around her, she slid out of bed and went over to the suitcase. She opened it up and pulled out some soft gray shorts and an extra-large T-shirt. Her hair was a wavy mess, so she brushed it out and bound it with a hair tie into a bun before she opened the door and padded down the hallway on bare feet. It was strange to be so comfortable in this house. She'd never felt this way in Chad's home, or even her own apartment back in Chicago.

Tantalizing scents teased her nose when she headed into the kitchen. Indiana stood with his back to her as he faced the island counter with the stovetop. He wore blue jeans and a dark-green henley with the sleeves rolled up, exposing tanned, muscled forearms. Her body warmed as she imagined his arms wrapping around her, holding her, pinning her down in bed... Oh boy, that was not the kind of thought she should be having.

"Don't worry, there will be plenty left for you."

She froze. How did he know she was there?

A soft little *woof* from the kitchen alerted her to who he was really talking to. *Jones.* The adorable mutt sat at Indiana's feet. His furry face was angled up watching Indiana stirring something on the stovetop. Indiana continued to stir as he turned to reach for a small bottle by the sink that held a fresh sprig of rosemary. As he turned, he spotted her, and his dark-brown hair fell into his eyes. He tossed his head to clear his vision. She wanted to run her hands through his hair, to see if it felt as silky as it looked. The need was so strong, her hands felt like they were almost itching with the need to reach for him.

"Hadlee," he spoke her name softly in that slightly rough way that sent shivers through her. That was how he'd said her name between kisses in the shower, as if the act of saying her name was a prayer to an ancient goddess. It made her feel ... honored ... cherished. Her heart clenched sharply, making her ribs ache.

"Sorry, I didn't mean to interrupt you." She glanced bashfully at the ground. She didn't actually feel like she'd interrupted, or even intruded, but this was his house, and they barely knew each other. How would she feel if someone was wandering around her apartment? Hadlee doubted she'd like it, unless she trusted that person.

A small smile curved Indiana's lips. "You weren't interrupting. Why don't you join me? Keep the cook company?" He winked at her and nodded at a barstool facing the stovetop from the other side of island.

She came more fully into the kitchen and Jones rushed to greet her with a furiously wagging tail and a happy huffing sound. He almost pranced on his paws, and she knelt, hugging him around the neck. Jones was one of those rare dogs that didn't just tolerate a hug but seemed to enjoy it.

"What are you making?" she asked as she settled on the barstool.

Indiana's gaze was warm as he examined her. "Meatballs. How are you feeling?" He didn't let her escape his gentle scrutiny. His eyes roved over her, as if seeking evidence of injuries the doctor might have missed. She knew she looked awful. She had bruises all over her face and arms ... and she knew she shouldn't have to care about dressing to appeal to a man, even if she liked that man. But the way he looked at her—not in disgust, but in gentle worry—it ... it made her feel like a person, not an object. Chad had only ever looked at her as an object and it taken far too long for her to realize the difference.

"I feel sore," she confessed. "Everything hurts. Even the bottoms of my feet." She grumbled as she propped her elbows on the counter and cupped her chin in her hands.

"I have some Epsom salts. Tonight you should take a hot bath in the master bathroom. I've got a good soaking tub. The salts should help with the soreness. Until then, I have Tylenol and you need to take those pain meds the doctor gave you." He fetched her medicine bottle from the counter and passed it to her before getting her a glass of water. She took a pill and studied the pot he'd been stirring.

"You said you were cooking meatballs?" She didn't see any meatballs on the stove. The liquid in the pot was a mix of purple and black blobs. Was that ketchup? It smelled a little like ketchup but also something else she couldn't place.

Indiana laughed as he stirred the contents in the pot again. "You'll laugh, but I swear this tastes amazing."

"What is it?" she asked as she leaned forward to inhale the smells of his questionable culinary skills.

"It's a recipe I learned when I was sixteen. I was working as a logger in Washington, and I was so damn tired every night that I had no energy to cook. I lived in this little trailer that only had a microwave and a small stovetop." As he talked, he removed a bag of meatballs from the freezer. He poured them into a bowl and microwaved them.

"You heat up the meatballs until they're hot and then you heat up a cup of ketchup and a cup of grape jelly in a pot. When the jelly fully melts with the ketchup, like this…" He stirred the now reddish-purple liquid, which was no longer lumpy but nice and smooth. "You add fresh rosemary." He leaned forward and handed her the sprig. "Want to put this in for me?"

She got off the stool and came around to join him at the stove. Their arms brushed and she couldn't help but be aware of how tall he was, how big he was. He wasn't too bulky in the way some men could be. His muscled arms and shoulders were large, but he didn't seem to have any extra weight on him. His hips were lean, but his buttocks were tight. Lord, she remembered that all too well, when she'd wrapped her leg around him in the shower and felt the steel of his ass muscles clenching as he pressed against her.

Face flaming, she plucked the little rosemary leaves from the stem and after inhaling their clean scent, she tossed them into the saucepan. The herbs added a new flavor to the aroma in the air. It smelled wonderful.

"Once the meatballs are ready, we stir them in."

Indiana passed her the large spoon he'd been using

so she could stir the sauce while he retrieved the meat-balls from the microwave and poured them into the pot. She stirred everything until the sauce covered the meatballs completely. Indiana opened his cabinets and removed two bowls and a large ladle.

"How many balls do you want?" he asked her.

"Four?" she asked hesitantly.

With a chuckle, he spooned six meatballs into a bowl and gave it to her with a fork.

"Now taste," he ordered as he leaned back against the counter to watch her try her first bite. Flavor exploded on her tongue. It didn't taste like ketchup or grape jelly at all. He was right, it tasted *amazing*.

"Okay wow, this is..." she gushed over a mouthful before she swallowed in embarrassment.

"Told you." He gave another throaty laugh and prepared himself a bowl.

They sat side by side at the kitchen table, enjoying their dinner in a companionable silence, until Jones broke the peace by pawing Hadlee's leg.

"Ouch!" She winced as his claws lightly scratched her leg. She leaned down to pet the dog and check the scrapes on her legs. Thankfully he hadn't opened any of her wounds.

"Jones," Indiana warned with a gentle tone. "Sit and wait your turn, buddy."

Jones moved to a distant spot in the kitchen and made sad puppy eyes at them. He dramatized it further by lying on the ground and letting out a heavy sigh.

"I take it he's a fan of meatballs?" Hadlee asked.

"You have no idea. He pays no rent or other expenses, he's a total freeloader, and he's spoiled as hell." Indiana gave Jones a mock scowl which only made the dog wag his tail.

As she ate, she studied Indiana, taking the time to really look at him without worrying about him noticing her too closely. This man had made her come so hard it had almost hurt in a good way. And he'd asked nothing for himself in return. She wanted to do something for him, to show how much she had truly appreciated what he'd done for her. He'd been selfless and compassionate with her, and she wanted to give some part of herself, however small it might be, to him.

"So you learned to cook at sixteen while you worked as a logger?"

"Yeah. It was a good job." He was quiet a long moment before he continued. "I learned to be strong and rely on myself."

Hadlee reached over and touched his shoulder. "That doesn't mean it wasn't hard or lonely."

Indiana's jaw clenched and unclenched then he sighed. "True. But I can't look back to the past and mourn what I couldn't have. I had to keep moving forward."

Hadlee understood all too well.

"Speaking of moving forward," Indiana said. "What are your plans for when you go home?"

She stared at her half-eaten bowl of meatballs. "I don't know. I sort of feel frozen in place. The second I leave Colorado and return to my life, things will get ugly. I'll have to deal with Chad's family, and face everyone at my job. They will know what happened. It's just going to get complicated."

The truth was she wanted to stay right where she was, in Indy's cabin, a warm mutt's fur brushing against her legs, and a sexy mountain man making her meatballs while she fantasized about everything he could do to her and how she'd beg him to do it over and over again. She'd always heard her friends joke about being with men who broke the bed while fucking them. Hadlee had never experienced that, but looking at Indiana? He was born to break beds, and she wanted to be beneath him when he did it.

But that would be hiding from her real life, and she wasn't a coward. She had survived something truly horrific, and she hadn't died. That meant something, didn't it? That her life was worth fighting for? She couldn't give up just because she knew she'd have to face some seriously uncomfortable situations.

"For what it's worth, Hadlee ... you're welcome here for as long as you want to stay." Indiana met her gaze. "I mean it. It's been nice having someone else here with me and Jones."

A flutter of hope blossomed in her chest at his offer. Perhaps because these moments with him felt *real* in a way so much of her life hadn't in the last few years.

"Thanks." Her appetite returned a little and she finished her meatballs.

"Do you want to watch a movie or something? You should elevate your ankle and rest. I can't think of a better way to do that than relaxing on the couch," Indiana suggested as he claimed her dishes and took them over the sink.

"That sounds fun. I haven't seen a movie in forever." She joined him to help load the dishwasher.

"Seriously?" He raised his dark brows in surprise.

"Chad never liked movies. He liked the news, and he kept it on all the time. I hated listening to the news cycles. It created a steady stream of stress, but he'd complain whenever I changed the channel so I just stopped watching what I like." Her growing list of things she'd given up on while with Chad was staggering. When would she stop starting sentences with *"Chad never...?"*

"Fuck," Indiana growled, and braced his hands on the sides of the sink. She gulped and stared at him, her pulse spiking. He was mad, really mad. She backed up a step automatically. When he noticed her small movement away from him, he tilted his head back and stared up at the ceiling.

"I'm sorry, honey. But that asshole treated you so badly I wish I could kill him again."

"Again?" she echoed in confusion. What the hell did he mean?

"Men like him don't deserve to be alive. That's all I meant." Indiana turned his back on her as he closed the dishwasher and let out a slow breath, the tension in his broad shoulders easing slightly.

"Why don't you get comfortable on the couch. I'll get some more water for you." He took her water glass and walked over to the fridge. Hadlee sensed he needed a minute to collect himself, so she headed into the main room and settled on the buttery-soft leather sofa and faced the large TV.

Indiana set a small plate of meatballs down for Jones in the kitchen and then he joined her in the den. He turned on the TV, pulled up a streaming service, and handed her the remote.

"You choose what we watch." He settled down beside her on the couch, about a foot separating them, but she could still feel his heat and it reminded her of the way he'd stepped into the shower and saved her with his kiss, his hands, his body.

She'd been spiraling with anxiety, and he'd halted the spinning by pulling her in close to him where the gravity of his very being grounded her and kept her safe, even as he brought her to an intense climax. Did he have any idea of the effect he had on her? Right then she wanted to curl up against him and take comfort in his heat, in his protective hold. But she couldn't do that. She'd just gone through Chad's horrific attack and then his death. Wouldn't it be weird for her to crawl onto his lap and ask to be held by a total stranger? A normal person wouldn't want to be touched, right? But she wanted him to touch her. What was wrong with her?

Indiana stretched an arm behind her on the couch but didn't put it around her shoulders. She swallowed hard and her focus drifted back to the movie selections. She wouldn't ask him to cuddle her, no matter how much she wanted him to. She would pick something tame, something sweet, something that would get her mind to stop thinking about hot showers or Indiana and his wonderfully wicked mouth.

He could feel heat rolling off her in waves. She smelled like sweet feminine desire. He wanted to wrap his arms around her and pull her onto his lap and feel comforted knowing she was safe and unharmed. But he'd meant what he'd said. She'd been through hell with that Parker asshole, and he wouldn't force any kind of intimacy on her. She had to ask him or tell him what she wanted him to do. But damned if she wasn't killing him with the scent of her need.

As the movie started, she was stiff and alert but as the movie progressed her eyes drifted closed and he took advantage of the moment to slide her closer to him and tucked her in the crook of his arm. He argued that he wasn't pushing intimacy on her, just letting her sleep more comfortably.

"Hmmm?" She made a soft, sweet, little sound as her eyes opened.

"You're falling asleep, honey. I wanted you to have a nice place to rest." He carefully put his arm around her shoulder and within a minute she was fast asleep. He let the movie play for another half hour before he lowered the volume and picked her up in his arms. He was going to put her to bed so she could have the benefit of a supportive mattress on her hips and shoulders. He knew from experience that sleeping on a couch when sore and injured was a good way to twinge one's back. Hadlee nuzzled into his chest before she woke when he was halfway down the hallway and gazed up at him with those sweet doe eyes, which were such a brilliant emerald in color. He saw no fear, no shame, just relief at realizing he was the one who held her.

"I feel so safe with you. *Why?*" Her voice was soft, breathy, curling around him, making his body hard with a need to take her to his bed and show her what a good man could do to a woman, what a good man could *give* her.

He wanted to tell her the truth. *Because you are my mate, my destiny, my gift from the earth, a creature to be treasured above all else.* But she couldn't know that, not yet. He'd have to find a way to tell her, but first he had to earn her trust.

"I'm glad you feel safe," he said instead.

He carried her into his bedroom, giving her a chance to ask why he hadn't taken her to the guest room, but she didn't. If she wanted him to, he would take her there, but he was unable to deny his instincts to put her in his bed, to surround her with his scent, even if it was just to sleep.

She let him lay her down on his bed, and when he started to move away, she caught his hand and pulled him back to her.

"Stay," she whispered, simply holding onto him.

"Stay?" he asked in a soft voice, wanting her to tell him what she wanted of him. He needed the words, or he needed some action to show she desired him.

Their gazes met and held. The drowsiness faded from her eyes and he saw a fresh, true desire sparkling in those emerald depths. She held her breath and gave him a nod.

A tic worked in his jaw as he tried to find some sense of control.

Without a word, she sat up and took her shirt off, letting him see her bare breasts. They were soft, full globes that called for his hands to cup and gently knead, but he stayed where he was.

God, she was fucking beautiful and yet he wanted to roar at the sight of the bruises on her skin. She pulled the hair tie out of her hair and a honey-gold waterfall tumbled down her shoulders in gleaming waves. He stopped himself from reaching out to touch her golden hair and instead fisted his hands at his sides.

A strangled growl escaped his lips when she lifted her hips, her eyes never leaving his as she slid her shorts and panties down her legs, leaving her bare. He swallowed, his whole body tensing, the nails of his hands biting into his palms. She continued to watch him, her gaze intent on his eyes, and she seemed to see whatever she needed to in his face. Then she parted her legs, inviting him to claim her, to mount her and take her to all the heights of pleasure she deserved. He could tell by her trembling that this offering of herself was frightening, given what she'd gone through in the woods with Chad.

"Are you sure you want this?" he asked, his tone low, rough. His bear was rumbling inside him to soothe his female, to show her she had nothing to fear and instead she had only to embrace the abundance of pleasure he could give her.

"Yes." Her voice was steady, and he trusted it more than the way her body shivered.

Her words set him free of the last bit of restraint he'd had on his own passion. He yanked his T-shirt off and his fingers fumbled with the buttons on his jeans. His cock strained against the now overly tight denim, but he didn't remove his pants. If he did, he'd jump her and fuck her wildly. She wasn't ready for that, not yet. His bear roared in displeasure at any barrier between his body and hers, but for now, he was in control of this encounter, not the beast within him.

Indiana gripped Hadlee's hips, being careful not to

touch anywhere she was bruised as he sank his fingers into her soft skin and held onto her. He slid her along the sheets so her bottom just touched the edge of the bed. Then he knelt between her parted thighs. His hands braced on the insides of her knees, pushing her open as he bent his head to gaze at her. Her heartbeat was faster than moments before, but it was from excitement rather than fear. Her feminine scent filled his nose, making his bear want to dance with pleasure. She held her breath as he took his fill of her, the pretty picture she painted for him, spread open and ready for his tongue to taste her honey.

Her legs tried to close, and he held them open as gently as he could.

"Easy, sweetheart, I just want to look at you." And he could look at her for days, memorizing the color of her, the shape of her, the scent, imprinting it all on his memory.

Hadlee stared at him down the length of her body, her face flushing. "I don't look pretty down there. I—"

He chuckled. "This is the prettiest pussy I've ever seen, honey." He knew that some men, especially human males, didn't like to go down on females because it was a selfless act of love that gave pleasure and confidence to women. Yet they expected females to get on their knees and take a male's cock, as if that was pleasurable for the female, when it wasn't. Sex was about sharing pleasure, about giving and receiving in both directions. It was an act meant for two creatures who cared for each other. Each side should give pleasure and receive pleasure as equally as possible.

"I need to taste you," he growled teasingly before he bent his head and licked her.

She was as sweet as any honey he had ever eaten. She moaned and arched as his tongue dragged through her slit and he suckled on her clit, teasing it out of its hood, which made Hadlee gasp and her hips jerk into him. He groaned against her heated flesh, his own body hard and aching for her. He knew she needed to come, and he wanted to be inside her when she did. He licked and sucked on her folds and her clit a few more moments until her legs were shaking with need against his shoulders as she tried to hold his body between them.

"Please, Indy, oh God please, Indy ... I need you," she begged, and the sound was a symphony to his ears.

He rose to his feet and removed his jeans and briefs. Then he stood in between her thighs, fully naked, his cock erect as he gripped it and guided it into her with one hand. With his other hand, he held onto her hip, his touch firm but soothing. She was impossibly tight as he entered her. The feel of her gripping him like a fist was almost too good to endure. He paced himself, drawing in and releasing a breath.

"You all right?" he asked.

She nodded and lifted her hips, easing him in deeper. He uttered her name as he pressed in slowly but confidently. Her eyes widened as he claimed her inch by sweet inch. When he fully sank in, his balls lightly tapped her bottom and he let out a shaky breath while keeping his control in check, barely. His bear wanted to mate her fast, to get her to explode with pleasure and then take his time for the second round, but bears and humans didn't always agree. And Indiana knew Hadlee needed a slower, more easy lover this first time.

"You still okay?" he asked her.

"Yes," she replied, her voice breathless.

"Good. Tell me if I do anything you don't like."

Then he started to move.

She moaned as he slid almost fully out of her and then thrust back in. When she took him easily, he grew more certain she could handle more. He leaned over her and braced his hands on either side of her face on the bedding as he watched her eyes while he made love to her. When she started to close her eyes, he stopped her.

"Keep them open, Hadlee. I want to watch you. I want to feel you take all of me inside you and come apart with my cock buried deep."

Her eyes widened in shock and her body twitched around him, clamping down in an involuntary spasm on his shaft. By the stunned look in her eyes, he knew she had assumed he'd be some sort of Boy Scout, but he was half animal, and sometimes he liked to fuck hard and talk dirty. He wasn't afraid of that side of himself because he'd never hurt or frightened any of the females he'd been with before.

"That's it, honey, give me your pretty little body. Let me *own* it," he whispered, and continued to fuck her hard. She nodded at him, her pupils expanding as she grew more desperate for a climax.

"Yes…" she urged. "Take me." She lifted her hips, meeting him over and over for each exquisite thrust. But she was keening softly with a desperate building cry for a climax just out of reach.

"You want to come?" he asked as he leaned more of his weight to one side so that his other hand could slide between their bodies and caress her clit.

"Uh-huh." She could only pant the words.

She nearly shrieked the second his fingertip touched her clit. Her hips shot up and he pumped deep, his pelvis hammering hers. She tensed, her fingers digging into his biceps as she came apart beneath him. The exquisite look of shock on her face had been worth the wait, worth her trust.

He came a second later with a roar loud enough to rattle the windows and doors in his house. His bear was close to the surface, more than it ever had been with any female before … because Hadlee could be his *mate*. Her thoughts danced through his head, making him smile as he struggled to breathe.

Never felt this way… Best sex of my life… Almost died… Want it again… Want him again… Don't want to leave this bed… Never leave him…

The breathless whispers teased his mind and filled his heart with a euphoric rush. Perhaps that was how he'd keep her with him. Use his body to love hers, until her heart followed. It wasn't the worst plan he'd come up with.

"Holy hell," he breathed as he relaxed on top of her, but then carefully rolled them so she was sprawled on top of his large frame.

She stared at him with eyes half glazed with satisfaction. The warm mounds of her breasts pressed against his chest, and it felt wonderful, so damn wonderful to have her lie with him like this, that his eyes burned with… *Jesus, are those tears*? The last time he cried was the day he buried his parents. He hadn't let himself open up to anything since then.

"Indy." She whispered his name so sweetly, so uncertainly, that his heart clenched. She cupped his cheek and studied his face, and he prayed she couldn't see his tears.

He swallowed and cleared his throat. "Did I hurt you?" He knew he had been moving a little rougher toward the end but he'd tried not to hurt any of her injuries.

The most delicious blush crept across her cheekbones and reddened the tip of her nose as she licked her lips nervously.

"No, you didn't hurt me. I'm worn out ... but in a good way." She giggled. "Does that even make sense? Maybe I do hurt but God, it feels good." She was almost rambling, and it was the cutest thing he'd ever seen. "I mean, I am as limp as a noodle and can't move at all .... and now I'm just sounding crazy." She cut herself off, but he continued to grin at her as he brushed a lock of hair behind her ears. She leaned into his touch and her eyes briefly closed as if his touch made her feel good. His cock, still buried deep in her body, twitched with renewed interest. She wriggled her hips in response, making them both groan.

"How are you hard again so soon? I thought you came," she said.

"Oh, I came, honey, so hard I almost blacked out. You were amazing," he praised her.

She moved on top of him again, torturing him sweetly.

"No more wiggling or I'll flip you over onto your stomach and take you again while you lie there," he warned, but his tone was teasing.

She let her chin collapse on his chest and closed her eyes with a little smile on her lips.

"Promises, promises. It'd probably kill me, but what a way to go," she replied, and then yawned. "You want me to get off you?"

"No. I like you right where you are." He shifted his body farther up the bed and she came with him, still lying on him like a hot little blanket. When they were properly on the bed with his head on a pillow, he pulled the sheets up over their bodies and closed his eyes to sleep.

He wasn't sure how long he had rested but when he woke, he used care to slide Hadlee's body off him and tuck her under the blankets. She continued to sleep deeply as he slipped out of the bedroom and moved through the darkened house. Twilight had given way to night when he walked out onto the grass in front of his home. The moon was bright with no clouds in the sky, and he could see easily through the woods. He breathed in the scents of the trees and let his bear free. The ancient magic of the change from human to animal filled his spirit with pure joy.

Soon he would not be able to change like this, not without endangering his life. He would have to abandon the call of the Earth, the pull of the moon and the song of the wind. He would have to be human for a long time until the threat of any hunters coming after him had passed. He dug his claws into the earth and his ears picked up on a sound. Huffing softly, he turned his large body back toward the front of his home and his heart jolted.

Hadlee was standing on the top porch step, the heavy throw blanket he'd tucked her into was wrapped around her shoulders and stared at him, eyes wide and face white as marble. She had seen him *change*.

Fuck, how could he have been so damned careless! Indiana stared back at her, unsure what to do as he let his bear slide back beneath his skin and became a man once more.

"You... Oh God..." she gasped. "It was *you*. You killed Chad!"

7

o, no, no, no...

Hadlee couldn't even scream, she just turned and ran back to the house... Into *his* house. The house of a murderous monster.

He was already back in his human form and surged up the steps after her. Abandoning the lock on the door, she fled deeper into the house. She couldn't let him catch her. She clutched the blanket like a shield and fled deeper into the house. There had to be a back door or garage door ... *something*. She pulled on the knob of the door at the far end of the hall, revealing the garage. The Bronco sat there and the keys lay on the dashboard.

Thank God!

She sprinted around to the driver's side, twinging her ankle as she leapt into the seat. The throw blanket she'd been carrying dropped to her lap, leaving her entirely naked. But she couldn't focus on that. She had to get out of there, *now*. The garage door was up so she hit the engine on button and threw the vehicle into reverse before she floored the gas. The car shot out of the garage at record speed, tires squealing, and seconds later she hit the dirt road at the end of the finished concrete driveway.

Hadlee pulled away from the house just as a completely naked Indiana came running back down the front steps, chasing her. She heard him shout her name, but she breathed a sigh of relief. There was no way he could catch up with the Bronco. She gunned the gas and vehicle shot down the road. She glanced in the rearview mirror hastily, seeing him illuminated in the flood lights at the front of the house, and then...

Oh god... He changed right there in the front yard. Suddenly Indiana *wasn't* a man anymore. He was a large brown bear. One she recognized with a primordial fear that was too ancient to ignore. He was the bear who had killed Chad.

It loped after her, his muzzle bared to show danger-ous, white teeth.

Hadlee sucked in a sharp breath, her lungs burning as memories assailed her. Chad's screams, the sounds of flesh tearing, bones crunching as he been killed, ricocheted off the insides of her skull. She gasped for breath and her body seized with a rising panic attack. She swiped frantically at her eyes as fearful tears blurred her vision, making it hard to see in the dark. When she checked the rearview mirror again, the bear was gone. She'd lost it in the woods.

She blew out a breath of relief and tightened her grip on the steering wheel. The car bounced and jerked over the bumpy road. Hadlee had no idea where she was going and had to slow down a little to see where to drive since all she had were headlights to show her the road.

As the Bronco turned around the bend of a thickly knotted copse of trees, a massive brown shape lunged out of the darkness into the road ahead of her. She screeched in terror and yanked the wheel sideways and slammed the brakes. Chest heaving, she stared through the windshield at the thing that had nearly caused her to wreck the Bronco.

It was the bear. It stood in the center of the road, its heavyset legs braced apart, its nose in the air as it sniffed in her direction. It had a wide face, and its body arched into an almost graceful hump above its shoulders, showing its immense strength and size.

She couldn't get around it, the road was too narrow. She couldn't go back because that wouldn't help either.

She was trapped. By a bear... A bear that moments ago had been a man she'd just had sex with.

The bear lumbered toward her, and she saw how big its sharp-clawed paws were. It approached the driver's side of the car. She hit the door locks and had a momentary sense of comfort when she remembered that even though bears could open unlocked doors, he wouldn't be able to open *this* one.

The bear was so large that his head was level with the window, and he breathed hard, fogging the glass with his black nose touching the surface. The eyes, such a light golden brown in the reflection of the car's interior lighting, were the same shade as Indiana's.

Don't think about him. Can't.

She shut her eyes and gripped the steering wheel with white knuckles. When nothing happened, she opened her eyes again and looked back at the bear. He was gone. Indiana stood just beside the door, his eyes fixed on her face. His arms were crossed on his bare chest, and he was scowling.

"Hadlee ... I'm not going to hurt you."

"You just turned into a freaking bear!" she shouted at him. Somehow screaming at him made her feel better; it let out some of the terror that had a grip on her lungs.

"Yes, I did. And I could talk to about that if you *unlock* the door." He nodded at the door handle.

"No way. You talk out there and I stay here in the car." She wasn't an idiot. She wasn't going to just open the car door and let this man ... bear ... man thing grab her and do God knew what to her. After Chad, she was never going to trust a man again...

He let out an aggrieved sigh and nodded. "Fine."

When he didn't immediately start talking, she arched a brow and waved a hand for him to go first.

"Right," he said, looking at the ground. "So I'm a bear ... a bear shifter."

A shifter? What the hell was a shifter?

"Of course, you wouldn't know about shifters. Fuck, I don't even know where to start." He dragged his fingers through his hair and drew attention to his bronzed, muscled bare chest. A chest she had lain on a short while ago after she'd slept with him. And she'd felt safe with him then. Maybe she was an idiot after all to agree to stay with a strange man in his house in the woods after what Chad had done to her. A fresh wave of terror crashed through her. She had slept with a man who turned into a bear. Was she going to turn into a creature like him?

Her breathing came too fast, too shallow.

"Hadlee? What's wrong?" Indiana tried to open the

door. He jerked on the handle and growled in frustration. "Let me in. You're *hyperventilating*."

As her brain started to fog, she reacted instinctively and reached for the unlock button, pressing it before she slumped on the seat. Her head was spinning, and her stomach heaved dangerously. Warm hands gently scooped her up and she was moved over to the passenger seat and eased into a position where she could lie with her body positioned against Indiana's bare shoulder. He was so hot, his skin heating her chilled flesh so much that she didn't care that they were both naked and huddled together. She just needed his heat, his touch. The panic within her chest started to ease bit by bit.

"Breathe, Hadlee." Indiana lifted one of her trembling hands and placed it against his chest. A steady pulse beat beneath her cold fingers.

"Feel this... Match your breath to the beats of my heart."

She closed her eyes, trying to do what he'd told her, to breathe with each slow, perfectly paced heartbeat. The fog in her head cleared after a long moment.

"That's it, honey." Indiana's gruff voice was a low, comforting rumble.

The rational part of her mind was still not ready to trust him, but her body, in its weakened state, trusted him without question. *Why?* That single word echoed in the vast chambers of her mind as she kept counting her breaths against the beats of this man's heart.

"Now, let's start over," he said. "I won't hurt you … even though I turn into a bear."

Hadlee's lashes flew open, and she gazed into Indiana's golden-brown eyes. She'd started to hope she'd just had a nightmare, and this was all still part of some insane fever dream. But it wasn't. She was naked, he was naked, and they were talking about him turning into a bear... A bear that had killed Chad.

"There are beings in the world humans don't know about. Shifters are one of them. My parents were bear shifters and they passed the trait on to me. We are fully human, but fully bear too. Two entities sharing the same body. When I'm in bear form, the bear is in control, but he hears me, feels me, knows all that I know. My bear would never hurt you."

He seemed to be reciting some rehearsed speech, like he'd practiced this over and over. It didn't hold a hint of practiced lies, but more like the feeling of someone finally confessing something to someone they'd been afraid to share for a long time. He must have kept this secret from so many people in his life and now he was sharing it with her.

He still held her hand pressed against his chest and

caressed her wrist with his callused fingertips. "I know this is a lot of information and you're not feeling well. But I want you to know the truth about me and know that I won't hurt you. I would never hurt you."

"But you killed Chad. You ripped his throat out and..." The words were too horrific for her to finish speaking.

"Had I been in human form, I still would have killed him, Hadlee. Because of what he did to you, a helpless female. In the wild, there are animals who turn mad, either by disease or injury. Those animals are dangerous, and the animal kingdom responds by ending their suffering. Your male was mad, Hadlee. He wasn't a creature who couldn't be healed. There was something broken in his mind and that made him deadly to anyone in his path. If you encounter a rabid dog that attacked someone, wouldn't you want to put it out of its misery and end its suffering? That is what I did. He can't hurt anymore females. He can't hurt *you* ever again. And once I was certain he was dead, I came back to you, and I carried you home to saw to your injuries."

Somehow his words made sense, as crazy as the entire situation was. When she'd been lying in the stream, certain she would die, the bear had come to her, sniffed her, and then, just as she'd started to black out, she'd seen something... A man. Indiana. Then everything had gone dark until she'd woken up in his home being tended to by him. He wasn't lying. He hadn't hurt her and even though she still felt like a logical woman in her situation would have run from him right now, she wanted answers more than she wanted to run.

"Why didn't you just stop Chad? You didn't have to kill—"

"I did." Indiana's voice was hard edged now. "A person who did what he did, who enjoyed the hurt he caused, who wanted to kill you... That is a creature who has lost his privilege to be on this Earth. This Earth was meant for good creatures, good people. Those beings who cause harm, death, and destruction, do not belong here. We both know the legal system of humans is imperfect. Bad people go free, and they often hurt others over and over with no consequences. I didn't want Chad to have a chance to get away."

Chad's screams still echoed in the back of her mind, but she buried them and focused on the questions pressing more urgently on her mind.

"Am I going to turn into a bear because we had … *sex*?" She lowered her voice and whispered the word *sex*.

A soft gleam of amusement lit Indiana's eyes. "No … I don't think so."

"That doesn't sound like you're convinced." She

tried to steady herself. "Am I going to turn into a bear, yes or no?"

"No ... not yet," he finally replied.

"*Yet?*" She yelped as he reached for her and pulled her onto his lap, banding his arms around her. They were both still completely naked and she could feel the heat of his entire body pouring into her cold limbs.

"I said not yet because the choice is up to you." He rubbed her back soothingly and tucked the blanket a little more firmly around her, not seeming to focus on her state of nakedness at all.

"I don't want to turn into a big bear," she whispered as fear slithered through her.

"Then you don't have to. But you could, if you accepted being my mate."

Indiana held his breath as he watched Hadlee absorb his words.

"Mate?" Her long, dark-gold lashes flew up and she looked up at him with confusion.

"In my world, we have true mates—other creatures that the universe has deemed to be our perfect match.

It's possible someone can have more than one true mate, but to find even one is rare and incredibly special."

He wanted to kiss her and give his mate comfort, but he knew she was reeling from everything she'd just learned. This was all entirely new and terrifying for her, like learning a new language, only his life and her future depended on her understanding it. He had to avoid overwhelming her by using his touch. Even possible mates had the ability to muddle each other's thoughts when the power of their touching got to be too much. Hadlee needed to be clear-headed to listen to him.

"How can I be your mate?" Hadlee finally asked. "We don't know each other."

"There are supposedly ways to tell if someone is a possible mate, the first being an addictive need to be near them and receive their touch. Think of it like a physical and mental fascination with the other person. And then there is the ability to hear each other's thoughts."

"Hear each other?" She moved down just a little bit closer to him.

So he held very still.

"Yes. When you were fleeing in the woods, I heard your cry of pain in my head. I told you to run, to fight. I didn't know it was you I was hearing at first, I just knew I was feeling and hearing a creature fight for its life and when you stumbled into the stream, I realized it was you I'd heard."

Her pupils dilated slightly and her gaze widened.

She remembers hearing me, he realized with quiet joy. Even in those moments of her terror, she'd heard him.

"I wasn't certain of this connection until I spoke to another bear shifter who runs a clan in Montana, and he confirmed what I believed I was sensing." He waited for her to react to his words, to ask him more about mates, but she evaded that talk with her next question.

"What's a clan?"

"Like a family. The females are the matriarchs, but we have alpha males that rule a clan alongside these females, their mates. The clans can be a single family or a vast community, but there will be ties, usually by the female bloodlines."

She wet her lips with her tongue. "You have a clan here?"

With a sigh he shook his head. "No, my mother was the last of her clan. When my parents died, I was the only one left. I had no connections to other bears. I roamed around, and for brief time I stayed with Dane's clan in Montana."

"Who's Dane?"

"An alpha male bear shifter who became a good friend to me. He's the one I called after I sensed my connection to you was stronger than it would be with a normal human female."

She shifted and he carefully tucked the blanket around her again as she shivered a little.

"Thank you," she murmured shyly, as if realizing again they were naked.

"You're welcome." It was admittedly awkward with them sitting there in the truck, her on his lap.

"Will you let me take you back to the house and so we can talk more about this?"

Please trust me, he silently prayed.

"Oh—kay." She said the word slowly, testing the word on her tongue.

"I won't hurt you. The last thing a shifter would do is hurt their potential mate."

"You won't try to force me to stay or—"

"No, of course not." He paused. "But I want to be able to tell you everything about myself and our possible bond before you leave. You deserve to know what this means." He waved a hand between their bodies. "It's an incredible gift, and while you have every right to refuse it, you deserve to have all the facts before you decide."

She nodded, as if accepting his suggestion. He slid

her back onto the passenger seat, turned the car back toward the house, and they rode in silence. When he pulled into the driveway, Jones was waiting by the garage and barked enthusiastically.

"Is he a shifter?" Hadlee pressed her hands against the window and stared at the dog with trepidation.

"No." Indiana covered his chuckle with a cough. "He's just a dog. Shifters are bears, wolves, any of the big cat species, foxes, and some wild predator birds like hawks, falcons, and owls. There may be other species out there, but those are the ones I've come across."

She continued to look at Jones but then finally she let out a breath and then opened the car door and climbed out. She kept the blanket wrapped around her and crouched down to give Jones a little cuddle. The mutt whined softly and wriggled nervously against Hadlee's body before licking her face, as if to reassure her she was safe here with the two of them.

Indiana hastily grabbed a pair of sweatpants from a storage cabinet in the garage and pulled them on before he followed Hadlee into his home. She settled on the couch, still clutching the blanket like a child. Jones jumped up to sit beside her and panted softly as he rested a paw upon Hadlee's knee. The dog had a way of knowing when and where he was needed most. Indiana sat on the edge of the ottoman and faced her, bracing his elbows on his knees.

"Ask me the questions you have. I'll do my best to answer them."

She pursed her lips in hesitation but then seemed to summon her courage. "So you've always been a bear shifter?"

"Yes. Shifters are usually born rather than made. We don't typically learn to change into our animal forms until around puberty. Sometimes a trauma or frightening experience can trigger a young child to shift before he's ready, but it's rare. Wolves are an exception—they can bite someone and make them a werewolf or a wolf shifter, but that is considered a crime in most wolf packs. Biting humans could lead to the world of shifters being exposed to humans who don't know about us."

"If you bit me, I wouldn't become a bear?"

He fought off a smile at the thought of how he'd certainly enjoy giving her a few love bites. "No, you'd just have a little love bite, but you wouldn't turn into a grizzly."

"But you said I could at some point change?"

"Yes. If a human mate fully bonds to their shifter mate, the human can learn to shift into the animal that will match their mate."

"How do you fully bond?" Hadlee asked in a small voice. "Have we done that? Become bonded?"

"Not yet. As to exactly how it happens, I'm not sure. My father once told me it can happen during a mating ... er, sex ... but a shifter will feel the change and feel the bond fully present. You and I would both know if we achieved a complete connection. It is said to be beautiful, to feel and sense that other soul connected to you by a thousand strings in the universe. My mother used to say it felt like an endless circle of light within her chest. For me..." He cleared his throat. "I would cherish finally feeling like I wasn't alone."

Indiana had been alone so long he wasn't sure what it would feel like to suddenly have her presence fully within his heart. But the idea of it lessened the deep ache in the center of his soul.

"Are you ... do you..." She struggled for a moment. "So you really want a mate?"

"Yes. I wasn't looking for one, but every shifter knows the value of a mate if one is found. They are priceless. If my possible mate wanted me too, I would want her with everything I had. Destiny, the Earth, the magic in a shifter's blood, they all help to choose the right person for us. Knowing what a gift a mate is makes it easy to accept having such a relationship so quickly."

"Do you just trust fate that this person is the right one for you?" She didn't seem to believe him.

Indiana slowly reached a hand out with his palm facing up. She stared at it and after a moment, she extended her own to place it on top of his. An instant flare of heat shot through him, and she gasped in return.

"*That...* What you feel between us is only a tiny taste of what pleasure mates feel when they are together. It doesn't have to be just during sex. It can be a hug, any squeeze of the hand or brush of our bodies as we cook in the kitchen or walk outside together. Mates feel the joy at the presence and touch of their kindred soul."

He closed his fingers over hers and held her hand. "Just feel me, Hadlee. Close your eyes and try."

She closed her eyes, and he gazed at her face as he spoke to her in her mind.

"*I would love you fiercely. I would cherish you. I would stand between you and any darkness in the world.*"

Her eyes flew open, and her lips parted.

"You heard me, didn't you?"

A strange, tender wonder filled her green eyes. "I did."

"Every word I said, that would be my mate vow to you." He still held onto her hand. "I want you to have time to think about this and have a chance to get to know me. Would you give me that time?"

"How long?" she asked.

"As long as you feel you need to make an honest decision. You owe yourself that."

She didn't pull away from him or his touch. "I could stay for a short while and see."

It was a small victory, but Indiana would take it.

"Good. Now it's time to get back to bed. You had a hell of a day."

She glanced out the window toward the dark forest which was almost invisible now because the interior lights reflected off the glass.

"Are you going to stay in the same bed with me?"

"That's up to you," Indiana replied. "If you want me to sleep beside you, choose my bed. If you wish to sleep alone, choose the guestroom. If you sleep beside me, I wouldn't do anything to you. If you simply need the comfort of my body next to yours, I would be happy to give that to you."

Her dark, golden brows lifted at his words and her lips parted, as though startled by his honesty.

"You might be the only man on the planet to say that and probably mean it," she said.

"Mates don't lie to each other. I will stay out here

for little while. I'm still wound up from changing into my bear form and can't quite settle for sleep yet."

He eyed her curiously, but he knew she was exhausted and needed to sleep. He turned on the TV and she rose, Jones dutifully following her as she walked down the hall. He didn't watch to see which room she chose. He wanted to put no pressure on her.

He sat back on the couch and watched at the TV. He was only halfway listening to the show he'd started watching when his phone buzzed. It was a text from Sheriff Wade.

Sorry, Indy. There was nothing I could do to stop it. Turn on the news.

He stared at the message and with a frown, changed over to the local news. A man at a news desk was speaking.

"Near the town of Aspen Falls yesterday, a man out hiking was attacked and killed by a bear. Authorities assured the public bear attacks are very unusual and hikers and other visitors to the area should take normal precautions, like carrying a large walking stick and bear mace. Local authorities advise against the use of firearms. They also remind everyone hunting is illegal in the area unless permits have been given, and there are no permits for hunting bears. If you see a black bear, please make lots of noise. This will usually drive the bear away, as they do not like confrontations with people."

Indiana winced. He hated bear mace. As a young shifter, he'd strayed too close to town once and had been hit with the stuff when a female jogger encountered him.

The news was treating him like a black bear. That was good. Grizzlies or brown bears were far more dangerous and often caused humans to panic and go hunting for them. The sheriff was doing his best to control the damage by telling everyone the attack was done by a black bear. He texted Wade back.

Indiana: You did your best. I appreciate it.

Wade: Stay out of trouble until things settle down.

Indiana: Yes sir.

He set his phone down to watch the rest of the news. After about an hour, he turned the TV off, got up, and walked down the hallway. He checked the guest room first. The bed was empty.

His heart leapt as he opened his own bedroom door next. Hadlee lay in the center of his bed, fast asleep. Jones was lying at her feet and his tail tapped the comforter as he saw Indiana. The dog, which mostly resembled a golden retriever managed to curl himself into a ball like a puppy when he slept. Indiana's chest tightened as he remembered finding the dog when he'd been only 2 months old, wandering the woods outside of town, starved, covered in ticks and exhausted. No doubt someone had stopped in town to abandon him and then kept on driving. He'd never understand humans, well most of them. He knew Hadlee would never have abandoned a puppy on the side of the road. She was all heart, his sweet little mate.

Indiana crossed the room, gave Jones a pat on the head, and got into bed beside Hadlee. He faced Hadlee's sleeping form. She looked less troubled than the last two times he'd had a chance to watch her sleep.

My mate... My beautiful, brave mate. He'd promised he would let her go if she wanted to leave, but it would kill him if she went. So he'd have to find a way to convince her to stay.

For the first time in years, his lonely heart held a spark of hope.

8

The woods were full of magic. The trees spoke in soft, ancient whispers born on winds from the north. Owls hooted softly in the growing gloom as twilight hushed the forest. Hadlee moved her paws through the grass, which was cool and soft. Her hard footpads absorbed the silken texture of the green blades. It made her want to rub her back against the nearest tree and rumble in satisfaction when she itched a hard-to-reach spot on her back.

The distant shiver of bushes drew her curiosity. She stood up on her hind legs, ears pricked forward as she drew in the deep scents of the world around her. A badger was near, and a deer had passed along the trail an hour ago. She had been alone in the woods, blissfully alone in a way only a creature connected to the Earth could understand. But she was no longer alone.

The bushes ahead of her parted and another bear, a grizzly, came into view, disturbing her peace. She kept herself upright, assessing him. He was male, and his dark, musky aroma drifting to her on the breeze was intriguing. He lifted his muzzle into the air and inhaled before he made an enticing, soft, tongue-clicking sound. She dropped down onto all fours and went toward him, hesitant but intrigued. His golden-brown eyes were warm, and as she came up to him, he rubbed his cheek against hers, then bumped his nose against her shoulder in a display of affection.

A lazy heat moved through her lower belly as she nuzzled him back and lightly nipped his shoulder. He made a huffing noise that sounded like a laugh, and she bounded around him in a circle, entreating him to play with her. He gave chase and loped after her through the trees until they reached a sunny meadow where he tackled her in the wildflowers and pinned her to the ground on her back. He gently set his jaws on her throat, showing his dominance during play. She pawed at him, growling and using her back legs to press against his stomach. He grunted and released her throat with another chuff, and she wiggled beneath him, her jaws closing around his foreleg as she bit him playfully.

Hadlee wasn't sure how long they frolicked before she rolled on her stomach and let out a contented sigh. He lay down beside her and rested his head on top of her shoulders protectively. His heartbeat pulsed against her back in a comforting rhythm. This was peace... *True* peace. Tears filled her eyes as a sob broke free of her throat.

Hadlee's cries woke her from her dream.

Yes, it was a dream and nothing more.

She wasn't a bear in the woods. She wasn't at peace. Less than a day ago, her boyfriend had tried to murder her and now she was facing the knowledge that there were things in the world she didn't fully understand, things that weren't real before yesterday but now were very real. She couldn't escape the fact someone close to her had died in a brutal way ... after brutalizing her. She was going to be dealing with that in her heart and mind for a long time. It had taken her years of therapy and self-work to adjust to losing her parents, the only family she'd had. Now she was facing Chad's death, his assault, and Indiana turning into a bear and her being his possible mate. It was too much, way too much for anyone to deal with.

Hadlee *was* afraid... Afraid of where all of these

things would lead her. After tasting the peace of that dream and waking to this reality, she wanted to curl in on herself and go back to sleep. She covered her face in her hands, letting the sunlight pouring in from the windows heat her skin when she got control of herself.

"You okay?" a deep, rumbling voice asked her. She jolted as she realized Indiana was in bed beside her. He sat up, putting an arm around her shoulders. She flinched at first, but didn't retreat from him. His touch almost immediately soothed her. He was bathed in morning light, his beautiful brown eyes so warm. His skin seemed to glow as though it had absorbed the sun and now he *glowed* with the light. He made her feel … safe, happy—just like the male bear had in her dream.

"Have you ever had a dream so wonderful you didn't want to wake up?" She could hear the tremor in her words, but she couldn't help it. She still felt too lost in the wake of the lovely dream that had vanished around her.

His gaze turned distant, as if replaying a past memory which both gave him joy and pain. How strange and yet fitting that happiness and sadness walked hand in hand. Without one, the other held no meaning.

"Yeah, I have." His voice was a little gruff, as if emotion choked him. "It feels like you've been cast out of some kind of heaven. You wake up alone, cold, missing what you had so much it feels like your heart is bleeding. You remember the joy, but it's followed so swiftly by sorrow. And you'd do anything to chase that happiness, but it's forever out of reach." He seemed to know exactly how she felt.

"What did you dream about?" she asked when she turned in his arms to look at him. His eyes were soft, and the same color as the male grizzly from her dreams as he focused on her face.

"I dream about my parents." He gave her a crooked grin. "We used to travel a lot every summer when I was a cub. Those were some of the best days of my life. We played in the lake, and we'd roam in the woods. My mom and dad would shift into their bear forms, and I rode in human form on my father's back. I was too young back then to shift but they let me come with them through the woods and learn about the life of bears. I didn't get to go to school with other kids. The risk of accidentally shifting was always too dangerous. But during the summer I sometimes made friends with the kids staying in the other cabins by the lake. It was safer to be in the woods rather than in the city. We could keep our distance easier."

As Indiana spoke, Hadlee rubbed her palm on his bare chest, listening to him and picturing those sunny summers. It soothed her to bask in his body heat, feel his skin beneath her fingers, and absorb the rich timbre of his voice.

He lightly fisted his hand in her hair and pulled her head back down so he could look into her eyes.

"What were you dreaming about?" he asked.

"Me?" she hedged.

"Yes, you." He chuckled as if he could read her mind and knew exactly what she was experiencing. She couldn't stop herself from running her fingertips down his arm, feeling his muscles leap beneath her touch, but he held still, letting her explore him, and she was glad he gave her such a freedom to get to know his body. It was comforting in the strangest way to touch him while they talked.

"Bears. I dreamed about bears," she finally admitted.

"Dreamed about? Or dreamed you *were* one?" he clarified, with a teasing glint in his eyes.

Somehow he knew what she'd dreamed.

"I dreamed I was a bear and I met another bear, a male." Her gaze flew up to his. "Was that you?"

He nodded. "I believe my bear met yours in a shared dream. That can happen with mates, even with poten-tial mates. We can dream about each other's memories, and we can dream *with* each other." He massaged her neck with strong fingers. "What did you think about being a bear?"

She gathered her thoughts before replying as she replayed her dream in her mind and how it made her feel.

"I felt free. The world felt so very big, but I wasn't afraid. My senses could pick up so much about my surroundings I felt at peace."

He nodded as if he understood. "And me? What did you think of my bear? We played together and rested together. Did you enjoy it?"

A blush filled her face when she remembered how she'd acted, letting him chase her and roll around in the meadows and bite his legs. It had been so much fun.

"I liked it," She nibbled her bottom lip. "Is it like that in reality? When you change?"

"Yes. My bear and I are together. I hear what he hears, and he sees what I see. We share each other's bodies. We are two entities bound together."

What Indiana was telling her was incredible. Only a few days ago she'd believed she'd known the world around her, but ... now she learned there were secret worlds with magic. It was hard to explain but knowing Indiana's secret was like seeing a wider array of colors in the spectrum of the world than she ever had before.

"This is…" She began searching for the words to describe the immensity of his world.

"A lot?" Indiana suggested. The word came out with a hint of worry in his tone.

"Yes, but not in a bad way." She trailed her fingers down his chest, and he captured her wrist so he could lift her hand and press kisses to her fingertips. The sweet action made slow heat roll through her.

"Just when the world was feeling small and gray, this makes it feel so vast and spectacular."

"It doesn't scare you to know that shifters exist? That there is a supernatural world full of things you'd always believed were simply fairytales?"

She caught herself on his words. "What other things? You mean there's more than shifters? You aren't teasing me?"

Indiana grinned. "Oh yes. They're quite real—dragons, mermaids, witches, warlocks, selkies, and even unicorns."

"You *really* are teasing me." She giggled and shoved him. "Wouldn't it be amazing if those things were real? I would love to see a unicorn."

"I'm not teasing you. Those creatures do exist. The world is just as wide and wonderful as you imagine. There is so much more I could share with you."

"But you can't tell me if we don't bond?"

"I could tell you, but it wouldn't be wise. There are also things in my world that would frighten you. If you choose to deny our bond, I don't want to burden you with the dangers of my world. In many ways its safer to remain ignorant of those things if you will never come across them as a mortal."

"Oh." His concern strangely hurt her because she craved to know everything, yet she couldn't agree to be his mate, not until she knew her own feelings. Chad had destroyed what little trust she had in herself and men. It could take quite a bit of time to rebuild belief in herself and her instincts. Would Indiana be able to give her that time?

Indiana pulled her close and she leaned into him, seeking the comfort that came so naturally when their bodies touched. She couldn't deny the heat between them, yet it wasn't simply a physical desire. It was *infinitely* more. His touch was like the caress of a feather's downy surface upon her soul. It was soothing, light, and pleasurable to her heart. It was *healing*.

"It's amazing," he whispered as he stroked a hand on her arm, his callused fingertips impossibly gentle. "Touching you feels like stepping in front of a waterfall and feeling the soft kiss of the cool mist upon my heated skin."

"Really?" She leaned into him, almost climbing onto his lap. She caught herself doing just that and stopped.

"Oh yeah," Indiana murmured. As he stared at her lips, he continued to stroke the skin along her bare arm. "It's like a drug... Touching you is never enough. I want to..." He cleared his throat.

"You want to what?" she pressed, her own eyes fixed on his lips, lips which knew how to seduce so sweetly, yet claim so roughly. His mouth was the beginning of all her fantasies. She reached up to trace the line of scars that ran along his jaw and cheek.

"I want to do bad things to you, sweetheart. My animal wants to put you on your hands and knees and pound into you, then after I have fucked you into exhaustion I want to hold you, to cuddle you in my arms and feel your heat against my body and count the beats of your heart. I want to teach you how to trust a male again, to show you how mating can be fun and wild, but let you know you will always be safe with me. I want so much of *everything* with you." He cupped the back of her head and pulled her into him another few inches as his soft lips covered hers. A warm light filled the darkness in her chest, like the glow of a firefly that pulsed softly in the gloom.

He moved his mouth sweetly over hers, coaxing her to respond, and soon she was wrapping her arms around his neck and surrendering to him. She moaned as he used his tongue to show her how slowly, *sweetly* he could make love to her. Heat, ancient and eternal, burned within her, demanding she give him her body and let him pleasure her in the ways only her perfect mate could know.

Mating was a female's world; it was a realm of sensation, instinct, and passion. Women connecting so deeply to the physical and emotional side of themselves was always looked down on. But the truth was, it was a woman's right to embrace her body and its pleasure. Hadlee had spent years holding her pain inside; now she wanted to hold onto pleasure, she wanted to feel like she could welcome her body's desire without fear or shame. All because Indiana was teaching her to trust herself again.

After a long moment, he withdrew, but he smiled as he stroked the pad of his thumb over her kiss-swollen lips.

"I won't rush this, not again. You should spend time with me out of bed."

"But I like you in bed," she protested.

His low chuckle sent delicious shivers through her.

"To consider me as a mate, you have to get to know me as a person."

He was right, dammit, but she wanted to push him

flat on his back and ride him until she couldn't walk for a day.

"Why don't we go for a hike in the woods. I want to show you something. Get dressed and meet me in the kitchen. I'll have breakfast ready for you." He leaned down, kissed the tip of her nose, and left her to deal with the still-burning embers of her desire. He closed the door behind him as he left, and she gave a frustrated huff before she flopped back onto her back.

INDIANA SMILED AS HE PLACED A PLATE OF PANCAKES IN FRONT of Hadlee. Then he filled Jones's food bowl with the dog's breakfast. Indiana had eaten a minute before she'd come out dressed for a hike. Now he watched with pleasure as she dug into the food. There was nothing sexier than a woman enjoying the food a man had cooked for her. Hadlee made an adorable little sound each time she took a bite, and his bear wanted to roll in the grass with the sheer pleasure of seeing her reactions.

As they ate their breakfast, he tossed questions at her, deeper ones about her family, the parents she'd lost, and even light-hearted ones like what her favorite drink was. He'd teased her mercilessly when she'd told him she secretly adored grape soda.

"My mother used to take me grocery shopping and there was this old pop machine out in front of the grocery store. She used to give me some of her pocket change and I'd be allowed to pick one children's book from the magazine racks and I'd get to run outside and get a grape soda. I'd read my book the entire way home and drink my soda. My mom... She'd look at me in the rearview mirror and I'd only see her eyes, but they always seemed to sparkle... You know how eyes can do that." Just thinking about her mother and those sunny memories made her want to cry and laugh at the same time. It seemed grief and joy were always intertwined.

He nodded and grinned. "She was happy to see you happy."

Hadlee's throat tightened. "She was. Dad was like that too, always had a big goofy smile and he'd create some little project outside for the two of us to work on. One summer I watched the gymnastics competition in the Olympics, and he built me my own ground-level balance beam to practice on in the grass. He worked so hard on it, and even though it wobbled a little, I practiced on it every day after I got home from school."

"It's the small joys we miss the most when those we

love have gone," Indiana said. He thought of all the times his parents had tucked him into bed, or when they'd chased fireflies on summer nights together. There were a thousand memories that glowed just like those fireflies deep inside his heart.

When they were done with breakfast, he packed a lightweight hiker's backpack with provisions and clipped on a collapsible water bowl for Jones. Then he, Hadlee, and Jones left the house and headed up the private trail he'd made over the last few years. As they walked, he pressed her with questions about her life, her favorite movies, the worst moments and the best memories she'd had, and people who touched her world. He had a deep desire to know everything about her she was willing to share with him.

Hadlee was thoughtful in her answers and always came back at him to answer the same question for himself. He found it easy to share about his life with her, about how he been attacked by a mountain lion as a young cub of fifteen, of the pain of healing and his shame at the scars. He talked about the loneliness he felt when he thought of having no connection to another bear clan.

When he shared about living with Dane and being turned down by young females for mating during the moon celebrations because of his scars, she stopped him on the trail and stroked her fingers over the lines. Then she kissed his scars, murmuring soft, sweet words to heal the last pangs those old memories held. He in turn gently stroked her bruised cheek and placed soft kisses on her skin. The gossamer thread that tied him to this little female had grown stronger and he couldn't stop himself from claiming her lips in a deep kiss which held them beneath the canopy of the aspens for a long while.

He tried not to think about letting her go if she chose to deny their bond. It would devastate him, but even fated mates always had a choice.

They climbed higher toward the distant mountains, and when he saw the fallen log ahead of them on the trail, he knew they were close. He could smell the waterfall; his bear senses had been keenly aware of it.

"It's not much farther." He helped her climb over the log and held her waist a moment longer than needed because he couldn't resist kissing her again. She exhaled softly, sweetly leaned into him so trustingly his heart ached. This woman had so much gentleness, so much compassion, so much love within her, which had been crushed and denied for so long. If she chose him, he would do everything he could to coax those parts of her back to life with his own love.

I would love you with all that I am. With every breath,

with every dream and hope. I would love you until I am but dust and once more my spirit flies free in this vast cosmos.

Hadlee lifted her head at his unspoken thoughts, hearing them in her own mind. He saw *everything* in her forest-colored eyes. She was time, she was space, and every beam of light and sparkling bit of dust in between. That connection, the one which would bind them forever, was a heartbeat away and he had to hold himself back from diving into the heaven of her soul. Not yet. She was not ready to bind herself to him, nor to have him bound to her.

"Come on." He curled his hand around hers and they hiked on until they reached the base of the waterfall. It cut through a patch of stony mountainside and cascaded down the cliffside to form a glittering pool below. The blossoming mist formed a half rainbow, which vanished into the trees beyond.

Hadlee's gaze traveled up the towering cliff face, tracing the waterfall's path, her face filled with wonder.

"It's beautiful."

"It is," he agreed, but he saw only *her*. She pulled her honey-gold hair back in a ponytail which bounced in the sunlight. Her eyes sparkled and she laughed in sheer delight at nature's wonder.

Jones bounded to the clear pool ahead of them, drinking in the water when he reached the edge. Then he splashed into the pool and swam around before climbing back out and shaking vigorously.

Hadlee turned to face Indiana, her eyes full of hope and curiosity.

"Um ... could I see your bear? Is it safe ... to change here?"

She wanted to see him so soon after being so afraid of his bear? It had to mean he stood a chance to win her over, didn't it?

"Are you sure?" He cupped her face in his hands, and she reached up to catch his wrists, holding onto him. She was gravity, her presence pulling him in like a cold, lonely moon's orbit around a brilliant sun.

"Yes, I'm sure." She pulled back from him, and she and Jones moved a short distance away. The dog was well acquainted with Indiana's bear form.

Indiana stripped out of his clothes, closed his eyes and allowed his connection with the ancient magic in the soil to rise. His body changed in mere seconds, and the grizzly bear stood before Hadlee. He scented adrenaline and fear coming off her, but she didn't move. She studied him bravely, her eyes sweeping over him.

"Indy, are you in there?" she asked hesitantly, and took one step forward.

He nodded his massive head at her and snuffled as he lowered his head and took two careful steps toward her. She held out a palm and he gently nudged his head into her hand. She gasped but didn't move. Her fingers stroked over his nose, up to his forehead and cautiously, adorably, she scratched behind his ears. He panted softly as exquisite pleasure rolled through his entire body. His mate was touching him, and it felt so wonderful. His bear was delighted, so much that it took all of Indiana's control to keep the bear from bouncing about the clearing like an excited little cub.

"You're beautiful," she whispered. Her fingers traced the scars that marred the chestnut-brown fur along his cheek. "Your coat has a bit of silver, is that why they call you a grizzly?"

He nodded.

She blushed. "I may have googled a bit about bears before we left for the hike. I read that grizzlies are brown bears but have a little more silver in their fur, and they live inland rather than in coastal regions," she declared with pride.

He huffed out a laugh and nudged her hip, encouraging more scratches behind his ears. The sunlight warmed his fur, and he eased down on the ground by the edge of the waterfall. Hadlee joined him and leaned against his right shoulder, her hands buried in his thick fur as though she was hugging her favorite stuffed animal.

Such an exquisite, stunning peace filled him as he lifted his nose toward the mist and inhaled deeply. The aspens whispered tales of older days when the mountains held no men, the stars fell from the skies and beasts held dominion over the Earth. *Long ago*, the tree sang, *mates were born when humankind was young. The beasts showed humans the way to unite with the Earth and the first shifter souls were born.*

The stories moved through him, filling his head with images, and songs. He passed it all to Hadlee, letting her see the bear's bond to the Earth, a bond she could have if she chose him and chose the bear.

A chilly breeze swept down the cliffside, teasing him with hints of winter's quiet urgency. They had so little time left for her to choose, but he could not rush her.

He rested his head on his paws. Hadlee leaned against him and after a long while he realized she was asleep. She trusted him so much that he she had fallen asleep against his furry side.

He fell deeper into that peace and urged the trees to keep singing their leafy lullabies to his mate.

Dream on Hadlee, dream of what we could share, what destiny can hold for us if you choose me.

9

Hadlee slowly woke to the sensation of soft fur against her cheek and the rumbling breathing of a bear. She opened her eyes, unafraid, the uniquely strange experience warming her heart even as the bear's body warmed her clear down to her toes. Hadlee glanced around the little clearing surrounding the waterfall. She spotted Jones snoozing in the shade nearby. Indiana huffed softly and lifted his head when he sensed she was awake, and he looked at her.

"Are you ready to go back?" she asked him.

The bear nodded and a moment later, a naked … very naked, and gorgeous man crouched beside her. She jolted, not from the shock of the sudden change, but from being so close to a naked Indiana. Was she ever going to get used to that?

"I'm sorry I just fell asleep against you like that," she said with a blush.

Indiana brushed her hair out of her eyes and grinned. "Never apologize for that. Females only sleep when they relax their guard, and that requires trust. It means you trust me and that is an honor."

He stood and retrieved his clothing. Hadlee tried and failed to look away from his impressive body, but not before she'd gotten a good look at his groin. She had thought he was big when they'd made love, and her suspicions were confirmed. Indiana seemed quite unbothered by his nakedness as he pulled on the jeans and T-shirt. Then he retrieved his pack and slung it over his shoulder.

"Ready, Jones?" Indiana bent over and ruffled the dog's fur. The golden-haired mutt licked Indiana's chin and bounded around Hadlee, barking excitedly. She picked up a stick and tossed it for the dog. He chased it down the path ahead of them, retrieving it and returning to them, prancing proudly as he showed off his prize.

As the three of them headed back down the trail, Hadlee was still full of questions.

"Am I the only one who knows? About you being a bear, I mean?"

"Wade knows." Indiana grasped her hand as she navigated a patch of loose rocks and steadied her an instant before her climbing boots slipped.

"The sheriff? How did he find out?" She couldn't help but worry about the law enforcement official knowing about the existence of shifters. Wouldn't that pose a danger to Indiana?

"Wade was out hiking one evening. A mountain lion was stalking him, and he didn't know it. I was following the mountain lion. The instant it would've pounced on him, I attacked the lion. Wade spun around and saw me, the larger shape in the darkness, and fired his gun, clipping my shoulder. I managed to kill the lion a moment later. But I was bleeding badly, and on instinct I shifted back to my human form. By that point, Wade realized I'd killed the mountain lion and saved his life, so he helped me. He got me to his house, patched me up, and called in the doc from town. He told her we'd been hunting a mountain lion and there'd been an accident." He paused in his tale to scoop her up, lift her over a fallen log, and set her back down.

"Did the doctor find out what you are?"

"No, thank God. Wade gave me some of his clothes to borrow and we roughed them up with some dirt. It looked like I'd gotten between him and his attempt to shoot the mountain lion." His smile was rueful. "Wade and I had a long talk that night while I recovered at his house. I expected him to be shocked, but he put a hand on my good shoulder and said 'Son, you're not the first supernatural creature I've run into. My sister-in-law is a witch.' I thought he was joking, but apparently he was serious. His brother's wife belongs to the Salem Witch Council."

Hadlee's heart sped up. "The Salem Witch Council? You mean witches are real and they live in America?" When he'd told her about the creatures earlier, she hadn't fully believed him.

"Yes," He chuckled. "Most of the witches and the warlocks are good, but there are occasionally bad ones, like with humans."

"So the Sheriff was okay with knowing you are a bear shifter? I mean ... you know, witches are one thing ... but you change into an animal. That's sort of differ-ent." She hoped he wasn't upset with her observation, but she was still trying to work out how she felt about everything. She liked his bear, now that she'd seen it, touched it. But she imagined a man like the sheriff might feel differently, especially since Indiana had the ability to kill people in his animal form.

"I get what you mean," Indiana said after a

moment. He brushed his hair out of his eyes. "Thankfully Wade trusts me. He said he doesn't mind me staying here at Aspen Falls as long as I keep out of trouble. And after that night, we've become good friends. The night that … the night I killed Parker, I called Wade and told him what I'd done."

"You did?" She halted on the trail to stare at him.

Indiana stopped with her, and Jones sat at his feet looking between them with a happy panting look.

"When I explained what Parker had done, what he tried to do to you in those last seconds … Wade sided with me. I didn't ask him to cover for me, but he did." He took a step closer to her. "Are you okay with that?"

Was she okay that Indiana was being protected by the sheriff for saving her life? Was she okay with him getting away with the murder of someone who'd tried to kill her?

He caught her chin and tilted her face up. She stared into Indiana's eyes. There was no hint of deception, no hint of warning, no hint of anything like what had filled Chad's eyes in those last minutes when he'd come after her. She saw only a gentle patience in Indiana's eyes, and a soft affection that made her heart clench. This man had killed to save her, not even knowing what that would mean for his own fate. Looking at it that way, there was only one real way to feel that made any sense.

"I'm okay with it. I'm glad you told me." She meant that to her very core. It was crazy. She'd only known this man a few days, but she trusted him, and he'd saved her life. He cared about her. He *valued* her in a way no other man ever had.

"I'll tell you anything, Hadlee. You'll always get the truth from me." Indiana brushed the pad of his thumb over her cheek and heat warmed her skin where he touched her. That simple touch seemed to ignite long-forgotten fires within her.

"Any other questions?" he asked, his lips curving into a soft smile that did funny things to her knees.

"Um ... give me a minute and I'll probably have a thousand. I just don't know where to start."

He laughed and the rich sound poured through her like fine whiskey.

"You're caught on the witches are real part, aren't you?" He captured her hand in his again, this time seemingly just to hold it rather than help her cross rocky terrain, since they were now on a smooth dirt path.

"Maybe just a little. It's a lot to process. Do ... um ... witches have mates, or is that just a shifter thing?"

"Most supernatural beings have true mates in one way or another, except witches. They can form a true mate bond to anyone they wish, so long as the feelings are returned. What's most interesting is that witches and warlocks go through an awakening where they need a truly powerful sexual experience, preferably with love involved, to open up their true power potential. It doesn't have to be with another witch or warlock, but it must be a powerful experience."

Hadlee couldn't help but think of how powerful it had felt to make love to Indiana, how she'd felt unmade and then reborn through that singular experience. She'd felt so close to him, and she'd felt … powerful in the most wonderful way.

"I remember from my western civilization classes in college that the old pagan religions believed sex held great power," Hadlee recalled.

"Indeed. The older religions were closely tied to the Earth. Magic is tied to the Earth, so it makes sense that the people in those ancient times would possibly have a better understanding of magic and its power, including how sex affects it." Indiana paused, still smiling faintly. "Shifters gain strength, of a sort, from mating. When we share ourselves fully with our mates, it's incredibly intense, and it can be healing, both emotionally and sometimes even physically. I wonder if that's a sort of power?"

Hadlee bit her lip before nodding. "It sounds like it. So, you've never … met another potential mate?"

"No, you are the first."

His words filled her with a flutter of wild excitement that she had to fight to hide. Hadlee still wasn't sure what she would do when it came time to make a decision, but a growing part of her wanted to leap into Indiana's arms and his world with both feet and never look back. And that ... that was dangerous, because the last time she'd leapt into a relationship, the man had tried to kill her.

When they reached Indiana's cabin, he let them inside.

"How about I make us some sandwiches?"

"Thanks, I'd like that." Hadlee went to the bathroom to wash up and when she returned to the kitchen, Jones was eating some sliced turkey in his bowl for a snack. Indiana passed her a plate. The man always had food ready for her and she really liked that.

"So about tonight—" he began, but a distant ringing halted him. "I believe that's your cell phone."

"Oh my God!" She had completely forgotten about her cell phone. She rushed into Indiana's bedroom and retrieved it from her suitcase. She flinched at the sight of over thirty missed calls. She slid her thumb across the screen to answer, even though she didn't recognize the number.

"Hello?"

"Hadlee? It's Beth Parker."

A bottomless pit formed in Hadlee's stomach. It was Chad's mother. She'd never talked to his mother; he'd kept Hadlee separate from his family as much as possible and barely mentioned them. He'd gotten so good at isolating her, even from his own parents.

"Hi ... um ... Mrs. Parker," she whispered. Her blood roared in her ears and her heart pounded hard enough that it hurt to breathe.

"The police just called about Chad. They said you were hiking when a bear attacked you both?" Beth's voice was shaky and Hadlee had to draw in a painful breath to keep from trembling.

"Yes, that's what happened." She held her breath, wondering if the sheriff had told Beth the truth, as he'd agreed to. *Please don't let this be a mistake*, she silently prayed.

"He also said..." The woman's voice wavered. "That you and Chad were having some problems and ... that he hurt you?"

Oh God, here it is. She had to tell the truth, even if it hurt Chad's mother.

"Yes, Mrs. Parker. I'm sorry you have to hear this, but Chad was harmful to me. It didn't start right away, but over six months, his cruelty became inescapable and when we were attacked, he was trying to choke me. I was just trying to get away and I was running through the woods when we stumbled into the path of the bear. I was badly hurt and lying on the ground and the bear didn't see me as a threat, but it saw Chad as one. So it attacked." She only paused after she'd said everything she had to say.

There was a long silence on the phone and Hadlee braced herself for the expected response. That she was exaggerating, that men had needs, that boys would be boys, or that her accusation would ruin Chad's memory.

"I thought ... I thought perhaps it was just me," Mrs. Parker confessed in a soft whisper. "Over the years I've wondered... Oh God. It sounds awful to speak of my child like this, but I don't think he was a good man. He wasn't even a good boy. I once caught him tying firecrackers to our cat's tail when he was twelve. I had to give our cat away because I didn't trust him around it. My husband thought I was overreacting. Chad treated me differently than he did his father."

Hadlee's heart stilled as she listened to Mrs. Parker's words. "Did he hurt you?"

There was a long pause full of pain before Beth replied.

"My other friends who had children said how sweet their kids were, and how they loved their mothers. But Chad... Everything he did or said to me carried this deep scorn that he couldn't fully hide from me. He played the perfect son for his father, but I knew better. I had proof that he was ... that he was cruel."

Hadlee could see the other woman's unspoken words. He had hurt her, and he left bruises to prove it, possibly even scars.

"I'm *so sorry*, Mrs. Parker." Hadlee hugged herself with one arm as the old pain, the old fear she'd pushed down over the last day clawed its way up to the surface. Her throat burned as she struggled to keep from crying.

"It's okay, Hadlee. You have nothing to apologize for. I'm the one who's sorry. I knew he wasn't ... safe to be around, and I should've warned you when you started dating him. I was a fool to just try to love my son no matter what. I thought perhaps if he met the right woman, she'd change him and take away that darkness inside of him." Beth paused, her voice breaking a little.

"We can't change men, Mrs. Parker. It's not our job as women to give up ourselves just to try and save a man who doesn't want to change. We can't blame ourselves unless we stay with them knowing they will hurt us. I was a fool too. He had me convinced I was lucky to be with him. He broke down my self-worth and my confidence. I felt so small, and slowly I lost trust in myself until it almost too late."

Beth Parker sniffled. "You're right. You're so very right. The sheriff said you were hurt, but he said you didn't need to go to the hospital?"

"It's just some cracked ribs, a sprained ankle, and some bruises. I'll heal."

Beth choked on a sob. "That's a lot more than just a few things. I'm so glad you didn't need to go to the hospital. I know you probably never want to speak to me again, but you have my number now if you need it, okay? You can call me anytime."

This woman ... this good-hearted woman, could have been a mother to replace the one she'd lost, but she and Beth would never have a relationship, like the one they both had imagined. It broke Hadlee's heart.

"Thank you, Mrs. Parker. I am really sorry this happened." She found herself apologizing again.

"Stop," Beth said. "No woman should take the blame for a man's actions. Chad made his decisions, and he faced the consequences. Your job is to get better, okay?"

"I will, thank you, Mrs. Parker."

After Hadlee hung up, she wasn't sure how long she sat on the edge of Indiana's bed until she realized

Indiana was leaning against the door jamb watching her with concern shading his face.

"You okay?"

"I honestly don't know. Did you hear everything?"

Indiana nodded and pushed away from the door-jamb. "I didn't mean to overhear. It's just hard to avoid, with my shifter senses. Even when I'm human I can hear, smell, and see better than most people." He knelt in front of her on one knee and took her hands in his.

"You're so cold, honey." He rubbed her icy fingers in his own warm ones.

She stared at him, mesmerized by the golden glow of his eyes, the beautiful lines of his face, and the heat that radiated off his massive, muscled form, which was so inviting. He was all brawn, all tanned muscle, and it should have frightened her, but he had only ever made her feel safe except for that first time she'd seen him shift into his bear. But even then, he had proved her fears unfounded. He had shown his sweetness, his gentleness, and his bear had become safe to her too.

"It's just..." She swallowed thickly as emotions tumbled through her like sands on a windswept dune. "I didn't think she'd believe me, but she did. Why did she believe me? I'm the reason her son died. She should hate me."

Indiana lifted her hands to his lips and pressed a kiss to her cold fingertips.

"I'm glad she believed you. Not all women think their children are perfect angels. She sensed something was wrong with him, just like I did."

They were quiet a long moment. She let out a shuddering breath and got to her feet at the same moment Indiana did. He must have seen something on her face that begged for a distraction because his eyes softened in understanding and he spoke.

"What if we went into town tonight to the bar and grill? They usually have a live band and dancing later in the evening. If you want to get some rest first, we can go later on and have some fun."

"That actually sounds nice," Hadlee admitted.

"Good. Why don't you take your next round of meds and get some sleep. We'll go in a few hours. If all we do is sit and have a nice meal, that's perfectly fine too." He kissed her forehead and left her alone to rest. Hadlee was exhausted, both from her hiking and from the gauntlet of emotions she'd just gone through when speaking to Chad's mother.

After she took her pain meds and antibiotics, she curled up in a blanket and closed her eyes. She didn't think of Chad or his mother. Instead, she thought of Indiana and his bear, and the way she'd seen him change between the two forms. His body had almost shimmered during the transformation, like magic. Because it *was* magic.

Magic existed. She could never go back to a world where magic didn't exist. It was a part of her now in a way that she couldn't quite explain. But it was there, slowly building like an electric charge in her blood. It felt a lot like *love*. Wasn't love a kind of magic?

Am I falling in love with him?

A small part of her forced herself to admit the truth in the dark, quiet bedroom. She'd never fallen hard or fast for anyone, not even Chad. Indiana had seen the real her, the hurt her, the vulnerable her, the scared her, and he'd held onto her when she felt that flood of panic threaten to carry her away. He had thrown out his arm and caught her, holding her fast, refusing to let go, and now he was slowly pulling her to safety, inch by inch.

She could *feel* him fighting for her to recover from what she'd endured. The quiet yet audible murmur of his thoughts was in the back of her mind, comforting rather than unsettling. Could she change her life forever, leave what she knew behind and trust in a future with Indiana? It would mean a life of secrets, a life partially hidden away from the world. And it could mean someday she could be a bear like him. A bear shifter...

As her mind calmed with the approach of sleep, she slipped into sunny dreams of being by the waterfall with Indiana, but this time she was in fur just like him.

INDIANA WAS STRANGELY NERVOUS AS HE HELPED HADLEE OUT of the Bronco and took her hand to lead her to the doors of the bar and grill at the end of Main Street. Hadlee had been quiet when she'd woken and remained quiet as they had driven into town. He felt through their growing connection that she was deep in thought. Her mind was slightly closed off to him, as she remained preoccupied by whatever was worrying her. He sensed that she wasn't closed off on purpose though. As far as he knew, a mate could retain some privacy by letting their thoughts sink deep within their minds.

"You still okay with this?" he asked as he stopped her from entering the bar and grill. Loud country music came from inside and he knew it might be too much for her.

"No, it's fine. I actually think I need the distraction." She smiled up at him. Her hair fell down in soft waves and his hands long to dig into the strands and feel their silkiness. She wore a cute pair of jeans shorts, Converse tennis shoes, and a loose, brightly colored teal top that made her eyes glow like jade illuminated by starlight. When she had first come out of the bedroom, he knew he would spend the night scaring men off because she was too irresistible.

"Then let's do this." He opened the door and let her enter first. The bar and grill was well lit near the front, where the restaurant and bar were located. It was packed with locals as well as tourists passing through town. In the back, there was a large dance floor with a band strumming their instruments. It was after nine and the place was already alive with energy. The bear within Indiana retreated deep, seeking to experience and feel this environment as little as possible. Bears were solitary by nature and his bear was no different.

Hadlee leaned against his side, and he put an arm around her waist.

"Are you okay with this?" she whispered.

"Yes." He wasn't exactly lying. He could handle this better than his bear could.

"Should we get drinks?" she offered.

"Good idea. They have some nice mocktails on the menu that won't mess with your pain meds." They wound their way through the crowds until they reached the bar.

"Hadlee!" Tiffany squealed when she spotted them from across the bar. "You came!" The sheriff's receptionist threw her arms around Hadlee, hugging her as if they were old friends. Then she noticed Indiana.

"Indy, you devil!" She hugged him too.

"Okay Tiff, how many drinks have you had tonight?" He patted her back gently, then released her so he could study the young woman's face clearly. He didn't want anything to happen to her; she was a sweet girl, and he knew how dangerous men could be.

"Just three margaritas. That's not too many, right, girl?" Tiffany asked Hadlee, wearing her best 'back me up on this' look.

"Three? Maybe we should have some water next," Hadlee suggested gently as she steered Tiffany over to the bar and ordered her a glass of water. Tiffany made a pouting face but soon she was smiling as she looked between Indiana and Hadlee.

"So you're staying with Indy?" Tiffany asked as she sipped her water.

"Yes." Hadlee's face pinkened adorably and Indiana had to fight the urge to pull her into his arms and kiss her when she blushed like that.

"Okay..." Tiffany was grinning, her head tilted to the side. "Got it, mum's the word."

"Mum? There's no mum," Hadlee protested. "We

haven't..." She stopped and glanced guiltily at Indiana. They both knew there had been some intense *mum*.

God, she was so damn cute. She couldn't lie worth shit and he liked that. She was open and honest.

"Oh, there's *totally* mum, girl," Tiffany whispered loudly. "No woman has ever stayed with Indiana before, that I've known about. Not until you. This is definitely *mum*." She patted Indiana's chest. "Good job, big guy. You picked a cutie here. She's pretty *and* smart." Tiffany winked at him and shot Hadlee a very drunk but genuine smile.

"Look, Tiffany..." Indiana began, his face heating up with his own blush when she kept mouthing the word "mum" at him as if it really did mean a nickname for sex, which it most certainly didn't.

"Look, girl, he's blushing," Tiffany cooed. "Jo, look — Indy's blushing!" Tiffany almost hollered across the bar, making a ton of people turn around and look their way.

Indiana spotted Jo, the diner's owner, coming toward them. She had ditched her uniform and was looking pretty in a sundress and strappy sandals. A tall, well-built man in jeans and a gray henley followed Jo.

"Well, look at you, Mr. Rivers, you are blushing," she teased Indiana. Then she introduced her date as

Alex. He shook Indiana's hand and gave him a quiet, polite smile.

"Alex works at the Madoc Ranch to the east of town," Jo explained.

"Oh? Nice to meet you," Indiana said. "I run a website design company. I live close to the waterfall in the woods."

"I've hiked up through there. Nice area," Alex said.

"How about you boys go and get us some drinks?" Jo leaned into her date and kissed his cheek.

"*Anything* for you," Alex promised Jo with a playful smirk that made the diner owner blush.

Indiana gave Hadlee's waist a light squeeze. "What do you want?"

"Just some water," Hadlee said. She wasn't sure she wanted a sugar crash just yet after she'd seen the list of mocktails on the menu.

"Be right back," he promised her. He followed Alex to the bar and was surprised to find Wade sitting at the far end of the counter. Alex ordered their drinks and Indiana nodded at the sheriff.

"Sheriff," he greeted Wade.

The law enforcement officer had a glass of whiskey in front of him and was staring into the distance, lost in thought. He startled when he heard Indiana's voice.

"Oh, evening Indy, what are you doing here?" Wade glanced around. "Is Ms. Wilson with you?"

"Yeah, she got trapped by Jo and Tiffany over there. Alex, Jo's friend, and I were sent over here for drinks. This is Alex, Jo's date." He introduced the two men as Alex carried three glasses of water and handed them out.

"Alex, nice to meet you." Wade nodded at the other man.

"Sheriff," Alex replied respectfully, and then handed Indiana one of the glasses for Hadlee.

"So ... everything okay?" Wade whispered under his breath. "Did you tell Ms. Wilson that the local news covered the bear attack?"

"Not yet. She got a call from Parker's mother this afternoon. That was all she could really handle."

"Shit," Wade muttered.

If they had been alone, Indiana would have told Wade that Hadlee now knew he was a shifter, but this was definitely not the place for that conversation.

"Oh," Alex murmured to Indiana and nudged him in the ribs. "I think the girls need rescuing." He nodded his head toward the trio of women across the room, who now stood at the edge of the dance floor. Four men had surrounded the three women and seemed to be trying to drag them onto the dance floor.

Indiana started to growl low and deep in his throat.

A hand suddenly grasped his arm hard, halting him before had the chance to charge over there.

"Easy, boy. Your bear's showing," Wade murmured, so softly that only Indiana's ears could pick it up.

Shit. He let out a slow breath, regained his control, and Wade released his arm. Then he stalked toward the men who were harassing his mate.

10

"Come on, baby, just one dance." The cowboy bothering Hadlee pulled hard on her arm. Her still-tender wrist twinged sharply with fresh pain.

"Ow!" She gasped and jerked her arm free of him. She'd managed to cover the bruises on her face earlier with makeup, but she couldn't hide her sore muscles.

"Hey, back off!" Tiffany hissed at the man and tried to shove his chest, but he dodged her and she fell forward.

"Tiff!" Jo lunged for Tiffany, trying to catch her friend before she hit the ground.

"Come on," the man drunkenly repeated, and tugged Hadlee away from her new friends the moment the other two women were distracted by Tiffany's near impact with the floor.

Hadlee nearly tripped as she was dragged out onto the dance floor. She clawed at his hand but couldn't dislodge his fingers. The man shifted his hold and released her wrist only to curl his arms around her waist, trying to grind against her beneath the dim smoky lights of the dance floor.

"Let go!" Hadlee snapped and tried to twist free of his hold. His touch felt wrong; not dangerous, but just wrong. She didn't want this man to touch her.

"One dance won't kill you," the cowboy complained. "And for God's sake, smile. You don't have to act so fucking uptight."

"Smile?" Hadlee's lips thinned. She was sick of men saying shit like this. "I don't have to smile for you, asshole. Let me go!"

"Or what?" He laughed. "You can't do shit. Now shut up and dance with me." He slid one hand over her ass and clenched it hard in his palm.

Hadlee swiftly brought her knee up right into the man's groin.

"How's that for an *or what*?" she snapped.

The man released her and doubled over with a cry of pain.

She'd wanted to come out and see Jo and Tiffany,

and she'd just wanted to dance with Indy and forget … forget all that had happened. Now she was forced to deal with this. Maybe it was time to go home. She whirled and smacked into a hard chest of another man.

"Listen buddy—" she started, but when she lifted her head she found herself staring into Indiana's furious face. Relief flooded her. "It's you! Thank God." She leaned into him, barely stopping herself from curling her arms around his neck. Indiana wrapped his arms around her, sheltering her.

"I see you handled things." He nodded at the man she'd escaped from. "Although I would've enjoyed throwing him out with the other *trash*." He glared at the man who took one look at the towering wall that was Indiana and started to whimper as he waddled off the dance floor.

"Yeah, I handled it. He was easy to deal with." It was guys like Chad that women had to watch out for. Men like him had ways of getting women to trust them first, and women never saw an assault coming until it was too late. The cowboy on the dance floor had shown his red flags early.

"Sorry I wasn't here sooner." Indiana's gaze roved over her body, searching for injuries. "Did he hurt you?" The way his eyes glowed with an animal menace for her, to protect her, warmed her heart. She shouldn't have been turned on by it, but heat rolled in slow delicious waves right down to her toes at the thought of this big, beautiful man wanting to protect and care for her.

"He didn't hurt me, not really," she said. "Thank you for worrying about me."

He cupped her chin and lifted her head up a little as he leaned down close to her. "Never thank me for doing what any good man would do for any woman."

Okay ... that sent shivers through her entire body. She wanted to burrow into his chest, but they were in public. People shouldn't see her like with Indiana, not a day after her boyfriend had been killed by a bear. It didn't matter that Chad had stopped being her boyfriend in truth the moment he'd started to destroy her sense of self-worth. That was the truth she had to face; she couldn't be in a relationship with a person who destroyed who she was.. She'd been living a lie while with Chad, and it was important she let that part of her past go as soon as possible.

"Are you okay, Hadlee?" Jo asked as she and Tiffany joined them on the dance floor.

"Yeah, I'm fine." She smiled at the other two women. They'd come straight to her aid without asking. She'd always wanted friends like that. It had been hard to meet people in Chicago when she'd worked long hours and traveled a lot. But Jo and Tiffany had welcomed her into their circle in minutes and... God, she wasn't going to cry, she wasn't. She blinked rapidly, trying to dispel the tears welling up in her eyes.

"What a jerk," Tiffany grumbled. "Most of the guys who come here are nice, right Jo?"

Jo gave Hadlee an amused look. "Most of them," she agreed. "Occasionally, we get a wild one or two, but most of the boys here will step in if they see a lady in distress."

Alex parted the crowds as he carried a tray of waters.

"You thirsty, Hadlee?" Jo asked her.

"I'm okay," Hadlee replied. "I think I just want to dance." She peeped up at Indiana from beneath her lashes and saw her brooding protector still watching her with concern.

Jo laughed. "No problem. We'll be in the bar, if you guys need us." Jo, Tiffany and Alex headed off the dance floor, leaving her and Indiana alone.

"You really want to dance?" Indiana's brow furrowed "How about your ankle? We can always sit and talk."

"I think I can manage a slow song." She nodded at the band that was finishing up their latest song. "Maybe you could ask them for one?"

"Hey, give us a slow one!" Indiana bellowed, making several people nearby jump.

"Sure, man!" the singer called back with a grin. He strummed a few notes on his guitar and started a slow tune.

As the singer crooned on about his girl being too sweet for him, Hadlee curled her arms around Indiana's neck. His large hands wrapped around her hips, and she stared up into his face. He was so gorgeous in that rugged sort of way that made a girl's knees go weak. She knew he seemed to be a little shy, just by watching how he glanced at other people from the moment they'd stepped into the bar. She wondered if it was because of the scars on his face, or from living alone out in the woods. Whatever it was caused by, she wanted him to feel like he could be himself with her. The lights from the nearby stage lit his light-brown eyes, making them luminous and golden like honey shot through with fire.

"So, walk me through this," she said.

"Through what?" he asked as they rotated in circles on the dance floor.

She licked her lips nervously. "Living here... I mean, I want to consider this." She lowered her voice. "I would need to figure out my work. I don't suppose your company needs someone in marketing?"

He grinned. "As it happens, I might. I've been expanding my services lately. I'm looking to do some online commercials on the various streaming services and on social media."

Hadlee could see the hope in his eyes, but she had to keep calm. It was crazy, after all, to consider leaving her entire life behind and moving here for a man who turned into a bear and claimed she was his true mate.

"Could you afford to pay me a decent salary?" She asked the question teasingly, but he responded to it seriously.

"I think so," he answered. "You think about it and tell me what number you're looking for, and I'm sure I can match it. My company has been doing well these last few years and I can afford to pay for quality employees."

They continued to dance, and she moved a little closer to him. "What about ... us ... this *mate thing*," she whispered back. "What does that mean? Are we boyfriend and girlfriend?" She cringed at her own words. It sounded so *teenage*.

"My parents got married; most shifters do have the legal protection offered by humans. That is something I would be honored to give you if you wished for it. But the choice of how we are together is something we decide when you're ready."

Marriage. The word used to offer her excitement. But after she'd started dating Chad, the idea of marriage made her nervous. When she'd thought Chad was going to propose, she'd felt ill and almost backed out of their vacation to come here. She never even thought about what her answer would be, she just worried about whether it would happen or not. But with Indiana, the nervousness wasn't there, and she was able to actually think about whether she wanted to say yes or no.

"I think with a little time, marriage might be a possibility." She waited for him to rage or get angry.

"Hadlee, I'm not him," Indiana intoned gently as he rubbed her back with one hand. "I won't ever react the way he would. Someday I hope you'll feel comfortable with me."

Oh, but she did feel comfortable with him in so many ways.

"I'm sorry. I know you aren't him. It's like he brainwashed me."

How long would it take for her to stop thinking of Indiana within the boundaries Chad had made?

"Come here." Indiana tucked her against him in what she now realized was a *bear hug.* It felt wonderful. She could smell the woods and the waterfall in his skin and clothes. He smelled wild and free, and his touch was all encompassing, and completely soothing.

"We stopped dancing," she murmured against his chest. She didn't want this to stop, this hug, this endless feeling of safety within his arms.

His rumbling chuckle shook her gently and she found herself smiling in response.

"Do you want to stay or go?" he asked as he nuzzled her ear with his lips. "We could go home, have hot chocolate and cuddle on the couch with a movie."

"That sounds nice." She knew her breathlessness was because cuddling with this man would lead to so much more, even though he wouldn't push her. She wanted it to lead to more.

"Is that a yes?" he asked.

"Hmmm ... yes." She turned her cheek so his lips brushed against her jaw, and he pressed a kiss to her throat. "*Definitely* yes."

"Let's go." He clasped her hand in his.

They exited the dance floor, passed back through the bar where they met up with Jo, Alex, and Tiffany before saying their good nights. As she hugged Jo and Tiffany, she realized she felt so welcome here, as if she'd lived here for years. It was strange to feel that way in a town with so few people, but she had instantly felt as though she belonged in a way she never had in a bigger city.

"Come by for brunch tomorrow at the diner," Jo called out after them. Hadlee promised her they would. Brunch at Jo's sounded wonderful.

It was nearly midnight when they reached Indiana's cabin. Indiana climbed out of the Bronco and suddenly froze, his face turned toward the woods.

"What is it?" Hadlee asked, dread crawling along her spine. She peered into the woods, but all she saw was black shadows, the gray ghosts of trees and sparse shafts of moonlight made murky under the canopy of leaves.

"Men are in my woods," Indiana replied, his voice barely above a whisper. "My bear can smell them."

"Men? What kind of men?" She matched the softness of his voice as she climbed out of the Bronco and joined him, both of them staring into the trees. Jones started barking from inside the house. Hadlee glanced back at the cabin and saw the dog's pale golden form illuminated in the glass windows facing them.

"It's hunters. Likely men looking for the killer bear they heard about on the news."

"You mean they're looking for *you*," she clarified. The blood in her veins was a sudden river of ice. "You won't change form until they leave, right?"

"I won't change," he promised as he put an arm around her shoulders. He turned his back on the woods and they headed for his house, but the tension didn't leave him. She could feel his muscles rigid in his arm around her body.

"Why would they hunt for bears at night?" Hadlee shot another glance at the dark woods over her shoulder before they climbed the steps to his front door.

"Because it's easier to find a bear asleep if you want to kill it. They probably have heat vision goggles to search for a bear's heat signature. It's also illegal to hunt bears, so hunting at night will afford them some protection against anyone monitoring the local woods. Come on, let's get inside. I don't want to draw them to the house." Indiana opened the door and suddenly Jones was a blur as he shot between their legs and raced down the steps. The dog dashed into the forest, vanishing from view.

"Jones!" Indiana shouted.

"Jones!" Hadlee echoed as she cupped her hands around her mouth.

"Jones!" they both called at the same time. The dog didn't return.

"I have to go after him," Indiana said. "Stay here, inside. Lock the door."

"No, I'm coming with you."

Indiana halted her when she tried to follow him down the steps by catching her shoulders. "I can travel faster on my own. I'm sorry, but you'd only slow me down."

"Oh…" she couldn't deny that his words hurt but he was right. He knew the forest better than her and could move faster and track them easier, thanks to his bear.

"Go inside, call the sheriff, and have them get out here as fast as they can. Wade can arrest them for trespassing since they're on my land."

She started to turn away but caught his shirt, pulling him to her. "Be careful," she whispered, and kissed him. He grasped her, holding her fast to him, his lips almost brutal as he kissed her back. An instant later they broke apart and he was breathing hard as he stared at her for a long second.

"I love you." He spoke the words softly before she could respond. Then he turned and ran into the darkness after the dog.

"I…" She didn't say the words that would have changed everything. She couldn't. Her throat had tightened too much to speak, so she fled into the house to call the sheriff.

INDIANA RAN TO THE WOODS FOLLOWING THE JONES'S SCENT. The breeze carried other aromas to him. The body odor of men, the smell of alcohol, the scent of gunpowder and metal.

Dammit Jones ... please be okay.

He leapt over fallen logs and halted as laughter carried along the wind through the night.

Jones's barking was closer, somewhere between the men and him. The dog hadn't reached the men, but he would soon.

"Jones!" he shouted into the darkness.

Jones barked frantically. A sudden gunshot echoed off the trees, seeming to come from every direction around Indiana. Jones cried out with a pained yelp and then there was only silence.

"Jones!" Indiana ran faster, his blood roaring as loud as his bear in his head. He could not change forms; he could not put his bear at risk, but he had to find Jones. The smells of the men grew stronger as well as the smell of blood. Indiana charged into a clearing and skidded to a stop at the side of three men standing over a fallen creature. *Jones.*

"You killed it, you idiot," one man grumbled.

"It's not dead. Its eyes are open and it's still breathing. Let's get out of here," the second man said.

"What did you do?" Indiana growled as he shoved the men away and knelt by his dog.

"Who the fuck are you?" one of the men snapped, and shoved at Indiana's shoulder.

Indiana ignored them as he assessed the dog's wound. Jones lay panting on his side, blood seeping from his left front leg. "Easy, buddy," Indiana crooned to his dearest friend and stroked Jones's head. Jones's tail gave a wobbly flap as he tried to wag it, but it dropped back to the ground and the dog whined.

He would have to carry the dog back, and he prayed that Jones wouldn't pass away before he could get him to the local vet.

"We should get out of here," the third man said.

Indiana whirled on them. "You're on my land. *Illegally*. I've called the sheriff. You're going to be arrested."

"The fuck we will," one the men said, and raised his rifle at Indiana. "No one knows we're out here."

"Don't Randy, let's just go," another one said.

The man didn't look away from Indiana, his eyes twin pools of dark nothingness. "No one will find this guy or his dog."

Indiana slowly stood to his full height drawing in a slow breath.

"Fine. If you leave now, I won't say anything when the sheriff gets here."

He could fight three men, but not a rifle. Every minute he wasted on them was one minute Jones didn't have to lose. He prayed his next action wasn't a mistake. He turned his back on the men, knelt, and picked up Jones.

"That's it boy, you'll be okay." He started walking away from the clearing back toward his house. Behind him the men continued to argue.

"He'll fucking tell, I know it!" someone shouted.

Pain exploded in Indiana's back at the same instant he heard the rifle pop off a shot. He grunted, falling forward. Jones toppled from his arms and landed with a whine nearby. Indiana tried to get up to his hands and knees. If there was one thing he'd learned, it was to never stay down in a fight.

"Finish him off, Randy," a man snarled.

A boot landed on his back, trying to press him to the ground on his stomach. He bellowed with pain, but didn't collapse. He was far stronger than these human males.

"This guy is a fucking monster," one man muttered. "Just shoot them and let's get out of here."

"Oh, I will." Randy hit the back of Indiana's head with the rifle and Indiana momentarily blacked out.

When he came to, he was fully on the ground with a rifle barrel pressed against the back of his skull. Despair, sharp and yet numbing, filled his entire body. Was this how Hadlee had felt when she lay in the stream, begging for help within her mind? She'd had no chance of escape. But Indiana had been there, he'd saved her. At least ... at least he would die knowing he had given his mate her life back, even if he could not share it with her.

"Do it!" someone begged. "Do it and let's get out of here."

The trees held a murmuring portent of a change in the wind, a ripple in the earth. Indiana's vision blurred as his bear tried to rise, but like Indiana, was too weak from the blow to his head.

A wild, untamed roar of a beast filled his ears. It was the last sound he heard before his grip on his consciousness slipped at last.

11

Hadlee hung up the phone and searched in the garage until she found a large flashlight. Then she tore off into the woods, shining the beam of light ahead of her so she could make out the uneven terrain and look for any signs of Indiana and Jones. Sheriff Wade was on his way, and all they had do was stay out of danger until he arrived. If she could find Indiana and his dog, she could—

Crack! A gunshot shot shattered her thoughts.

"Indy!" she screamed, and started moving fast, frantic. She slipped and tripped over rocks and roots, tearing the skin on her knees as she landed on the ground. Hadlee grasped the flashlight, got up, ignoring the pain, and continued onward.

Can't stop. Have to find them. The mantra ran over

and over in her head, driving her forward into the dark woods.

She pushed away the pain of her sore body and the stinging cuts and kept moving. The second gunshot nearly ripped her heart from her chest in sheer shock. Figures emerged from the gloom up ahead. She swung the flashlight beam in that direction and spotted Indy lying on the ground, a man pressing a boot to the back of his shoulders and aiming a rifle at the back of his head.

"No..." The single word escaped her with a pained moaned before it turned into a howl of rage.

It had to stop... This endless violence... This cruelty.

I have to stop it. The thoughts were so loud in her head they seemed to echo off the distant mountains and shake the forest.

Hadlee moved without thought, her body leaning into ancient instincts as she charged the men. She flung the flashlight away, the beam of light spiraling in sharp flashes off the nearest trees. But Hadlee focused only on the threat before her that must be eliminated.

I will stop them. I will protect my mate. Those words seemed to roar from a deep cavern within her chest which held the secrets of the unquenchable flame within her heart. It beat a rhythm that could never be stopped. She would burn on this night. She would burn up the world to save the man she loved.

Hadlee... Her name whispered among the ghostly branches of the birches and quivered within the hollows of the oldest oaks. Time seemed to slow down, the men before her almost unmoving as she listened to the forest.

Would you save him? Would you claim him?

The trees were calling her name, offering her the power to save Indiana.

Yes ... she breathed back, drawing in the scents of the earth and the sky, letting it fuel her inner fire.

She accepted the power, promised any price she'd have to pay to save the man she loved, the man that she'd been unable to say the words to. Now she would *show* him her love.

Her clothing tightened, her body strained, every muscle and bone moved out of place and then ... freedom came with *fur*. Sharp new senses exploded around her: the tangy smell of blood, the acrid smell of gunpowder, and male human sweat. She processed it all in a matter of seconds as she surged across the clearing and attacked.

Her paws struck flesh, her claws dug deep into bone. She was bathed in the terrified screams of the human men as she protected what belonged to her.

When the screaming stopped, when the bodies on the ground ceased to move, she panted and swung her head about, confused as the battle lust faded. Who ... who was she? *Where* was she? She sniffed the wind, listened to the trees, which sung of safety in the distant mountains if only she could run away. She turned her back upon the clearing and huffed uncertainly as she eyed the mountains.

Run ... run away, her instincts told her. *Flee this place. Flee the humans.*

But she couldn't. Something kept her here, some cosmic pull that was too great for any name. She turned to face the clearing again and saw a human male's body that didn't smell bad to her. It smelled good, welcoming, despite the fact that it also smelled of blood. Cautiously she wandered her way over to him and nudged the man's face with her snout. He let out a soft groan, which drew a growl from her. The male was alive. What should she do? Was he a threat? No ... he wasn't. But what was he to her, if not a threat?

"Hadlee?" The man spoke a word. A word that she felt she was supposed to know. It tugged at her mind, calling her to remember.

"Holy shit!" Another human appeared from behind her. She whirled and snarled at the newcomer, barring her teeth and ready to charge. This man held a gun raised at her, but he didn't fire.

"Indy, what the hell's going on?" the man shouted hit as his gaze darted between her and the male on the ground.

"Wade ... don't shoot her. It's ... Hadlee." The man on the ground groaned as he struggled for words.

The bear tilted her head at the odd words strung together. Her ... Hadlee. Was *she* Hadlee?

The man near her reached for her paw, and she stared at his very human hand covered in blood as he gripped her claws. Rather than pull away, she studied him closely, inhaling his scent again, the scent that made her want to roll about in the grass in sunlight. His golden-brown eyes lifted to hers and even though they were full of pain, she saw an infinite universe within them. A universe that held her face ... her *human* face.

"Come back to me, honey. Let go of the wild. Let go of your bear." It seemed like every word cost him, but his voice... Oh how she adored the sound of it, even though he was clearly in pain.

Leave the bear? But she was the bear, wasn't she? How could she leave herself?

"I'm here, Hadlee. Let go of your bear and come back to me." His grip on her paw tightened.

She turned her head once more to the hills and

breathed in the wild scent of the mountains beyond. Then she let out that breath and from one second to the next, she changed. Naked, cold, trembling violently, she fell to her knees beside Indiana.

"Dammit!" Wade cursed as he rushed over to them. He shrugged out of his sheriff jacket and draped it over Hadlee's shoulders. She stared down at her blood-soaked hands that shook in the wan moonlight.

Why was she covered in blood? *Death*. Hadlee felt a wave of nausea force its way up. She vomited as the smells of death came to her on the breeze. Death that she had caused. She'd killed someone. More than one someone.

"Wade, check on Jones, they shot him." Indiana tried to push away the sheriff's hands as the man attempted to examine him.

"Your dog will live. It's you I'm worried about," Wade snapped. "It looks like someone shot you."

"Someone did," Indiana groaned.

"Indy?" Hadlee choked on his name as she fully realized what she had done. She had killed three men to save him. She had murdered those men. But they'd been about to kill him.

"It's okay," Indiana murmured as he struggled to sit up. "You're going to be okay, honey," he said as Wade helped him lean against a nearby tree.

"Looks like the bullet went clear through your shoulder," Wade said as he knelt by Indiana and studied the wounds. I don't think we'll have to dig a bullet out. Can you walk?"

Indiana huffed out a laugh. "Yeah, I can if I need to. Can you carry Jones?"

"I can. My patrol car isn't far."

Hadlee struggled to stand, and Indiana reached for her. A current of heat instantly rippled through her as she and her mate leaned against one another for support.

"Put your arm around me," she whispered to him, and she felt some of her strength returning when she touched him. He did as she asked, and they followed behind Sheriff Wade who picked up the injured dog and cradled it in his arms.

As they got into the sheriff's car, she stared at the woods, her mind going over what she'd done. She kept seeing the men's faces, hearing their screams, tasting their blood. It was a horror movie that wouldn't stop replaying in her head.

"Hey..." Indiana tucked her against his body. "You're okay," he whispered as he pressed a gentle kiss to her temple. "You're okay now."

But she wasn't. She'd killed people. She was no better than Chad.

"I've texted the doctor. I also contacted the vet," Wade said from the front seat. "They'll be ready for us when we get into town."

"We're going into town?" Hadlee asked.

"'Fraid so. I have to explain the bodies somehow, and Indiana needs treatment on that wound immediately."

Bodies. Hadlee flinched at the word and closed her eyes as tears fell down her cheeks. She tried to master her thoughts during the drive. Twenty minutes later, the sheriff parked his car behind the back of the vet clinic. A vet and two technicians rushed out to meet them. Jones was carefully lifted out of the back of the car and carried inside.

"I need go with him," Indiana muttered as he tried to open the car door and get out. Hadlee curled her hands in his blood-soaked shirt and held onto him, keeping him where he was.

"I can go for you. You need to see the doctor. You're still bleeding, I can smell it," she said. His blood scented the air so thickly, making the bear in the back of her mind growl in distress.

"Honey, as much as I love you for wanting to do that, you can't. You don't have any clothes on," Indiana whispered.

Only then did she realize she was naked. The sheriff's coat was zipped up around her. She hadn't even remembered putting her arms in the sleeves. When had that happened? Indiana must have done it. Faint traces of his blood streaked across parts of the brown canvas coat.

"Okay, Indy. You're next. Let's get you inside and I'll find some clothes for Miss Wilson so she can stay with you while the doc looks you over."

Wade drove down the street to the medical clinic, and he and Indiana got out, leaving Hadlee alone in the dark squad car. She let out a shuddering breath as she tried to ignore the tangy scent of blood. She could smell it far more clearly now than she did as a human. Because she wasn't fully human any longer. She was a shifter, like Indiana. She'd become a bear.

Hadlee had been so lost in thought about what she'd done, she hadn't fully processed the fact that she'd shifted into a brown bear. She'd accepted the call of the wild that the trees had given her. She had fully mated herself to Indiana in that moment when he had needed her. Hadlee had saved his life and changed her own, all in an instant. The enormity of that realization stunned her.

A figure came toward the car in the dark and she relaxed when she realized it was the sheriff. He opened the back door of the SUV and handed her a pair of sweats and a sweatshirt, as well as a pair of boots.

"Put these on and then we'll check on Indy."

He waited for her to change, and they walked up to the back door to the clinic together. Just before he opened the door, he turned to face her, his features half-lit by the fluorescent lights above the back door.

"I won't tell anyone about what you are," he breathed. "But if you stay here with Indy, you have to learn to control yourself. No more killing." He wiped a hand over his face. "I know those men deserved it, but I can't protect either of you if this keeps happening."

Tears coated her face. "I didn't want to kill them. I just reacted when I saw them shoot Indy. I didn't even mean to ... shift. I was fully human until the instant before I changed..."

"So you aren't like Indy then? I mean, you weren't born that way? I thought you were human, but to see you change from bear to woman, well I figured maybe I'd missed something, and you were a shifter like him."

"No, I was human. But Indiana warned me that I could shift if I..." She sucked in a sharp breath and clutched the thick sweatshirt around her shaking body.

"If what?" Wade pressed.

"If I fully accepted the true mate bond to him. It would make me be able to shift."

"True mates." The sheriff sighed and gave her a soft look of understanding. "I've heard about that, never seen it though." He studied her with more curiosity than concern. "I've heard it's a powerful thing, driven by instinct—"

Indiana's curses suddenly filled her head, distracting her from what the sheriff was saying. Indiana was in pain and the thin veil between their minds was weaker than ever, letting her hear and feel the knife-like pain in his upper body.

"Indy's hurt!" She pushed the sheriff out of the way and grabbed the door handle, wrenching it open so hard it banged against the outer wall of the clinic. She found him in an exam room with two nurses and Dr. Ravenwood attending him. He was shirtless, and the nurses were cleaning the gunshot wounds on the front and back of his body.

"We need to pack both wounds with antibiotics and seal them with bandages. I think a few stitches would be good to help keep them closed," Dr. Ravenwood explained to Indiana.

Indy muttered his agreement and seemed to sense Hadlee's presence in the doorway. His gaze pulled away from the medical staff and he stared at her.

You okay? Her question went through the bond in her mind to him. She could feel the words travel upon a glittering path straight to him. It was beautiful ... peaceful ... and so *real*, realer than anything she'd ever felt.

Yeah, the cleaning hurt like hell but I'll be okay. After his silent reply, he held out a hand and she rushed over to him. She clasped her fingers in his and oh God, the instant comfort of their physical connection was immediate. She pressed her lips to his bare shoulder in a kiss and he squeezed her fingers tighter.

"Miss Wilson, the sheriff didn't mention you were injured. Do you need me to look at anything?" Dr. Ravenwood asked as she finished the stitches on Indiana's back.

Hadlee shook her head, still clutching Indiana's hand. "I'm fine."

"Sheriff, have you called the coroner yet?" Dr. Ravenwood asked Wade as he joined them in the exam room.

"Yep, they'll be out to the scene in half an hour. I am just waiting to escort these two home when you're done. Then I'm heading over there."

"Indiana will be done in a few minutes and I can release him," the doctor added as she peered down at Indiana's skin and added another stich. He stiffened and Hadlee held tighter to him.

"I'll wait by the car out back." The sheriff nodded at

the pair of them and left the exam room. Hadlee settled in beside Indiana.

His wounds were already healing. Indiana could feel the skin slowly knitting together in the healing way of all shifters. The quickness of it was in part due to his mate. His true mate, one fully bonded to him, now sat beside him, her fingers interlinked with his. Her strength, her love, came through the bond like electricity, firing his cells into hyper-healing.

Indiana was careful not to bother Hadlee with his thoughts, not until she got used to their deeper, stronger connection. But he had so many things he wanted to ask her about what had happened tonight. Yet he couldn't even ask one question because they weren't alone.

"All done, Mr. Rivers," the doctor said. A nurse handed him his discharge papers along with wound care instructions. He promised to come back to the clinic in a few days to have the wounds checked and stitches removed.

As they exited the back of the clinic where Wade

waited with his patrol SUV, Indiana put an arm around Hadlee's waist and pulled her close to whisper.

"When we're alone, we'll talk."

"All right," she agreed.

Wade took them to the vet clinic so they could check on Jones. The vet had put the dog under to remove the bullet and did his best to stabilize the injury with a cast on the dog's leg. Jones would be staying at the vet for a few more days for monitoring before he'd be allowed to go home and rest. Indiana bent over the sleeping dog on the surgery table, gently stroked the dog's head, and whispered his love in the dog's ear. Hadlee did the same, her sweet tears wetting the dog's head as she kissed him.

"Get well, we will bring you home soon," Hadlee promised Jones, and kissed his head again.

Indiana's heart quivered with a desperate joy at the way she had said *we*.

Everyone was exhausted when the sheriff stopped his car in front of Indiana's home.

"It's been a hell of a night," Wade muttered as he followed Indiana and Hadlee up the steps up to Indiana's front door. The front door was still half open from Jones's earlier escape.

"Will you need our statements tonight?" Indiana asked Wade.

"No, we'll cover that tomorrow. I'll handle the scene tonight," Wade said quietly. "I'm going to tell the news station tomorrow morning I was able to hunt down and kill the bear. That should keep men away from your woods."

"Thank you." Indiana shook Wade's hand. The sheriff had done more for him than he ever imagined the man would. Indiana was lucky to call him a friend.

"Just remember … no more bodies, either of you." Wade looked at Hadlee a little longer and she ducked her head.

"We promise, no more bodies," Indiana vowed. If he had to build a fence around his lands, he would do it; anything to keep men away from his sanctuary. But he would start with a good fence around the yard for Jones, to make sure the dog wouldn't run out into the night again. They'd never had trouble like this before, but they'd also never had strange men in the woods. Jones was well trained, but Indiana knew better than most people that when instincts took over, it was almost impossible to stop a creature from following them.

"I'll be back later tomorrow, and we'll work out the details of what happened and how best to handle the situation."

"Thanks, Wade." Indiana waved goodbye to Wade.

When he and Hadlee were alone, Indiana locked the door and walked into the kitchen to get a glass of water. She lingered in the kitchen doorway, her arms wrapped around her body. He held out a water glass and she came toward him to take it, drinking it gratefully. She set the glass down on the counter and stared at him. Her large green eyes were dark, like a forest at midnight; so beautiful and yet so solemn.

"Indy ... I *changed*," she whispered, her body trembling again.

"I know," he murmured and opened his arms to her.

She walked into his embrace and buried her face against his chest.

"It's okay," he whispered. Her world had changed forever.

"When I saw you hurt ... I heard the trees singing to me," she whispered.

"What did they ask you?" He smoothed a hand over her hair, stroking her, and she let out a shuddering sigh.

"They asked if I loved you ... if I would do anything to save you. I didn't even think. I just said yes. I would pay any price."

She lifted her face up and he stared down at the miracle in his arms. In the moment that he lay dying, she'd chosen him.

He had to force his voice to be calm before he was able to speak.

"I love you, Hadlee Wilson. I know you didn't come here expecting to find me or this life, but I promise you that until my last breath, you have my love, my protection, and my respect. My *everything*."

Those lovely green eyes of hers misted with tears.

"I never thought I could jump into love like this … but you were right," she said. "In the moment that mattered, there was only one choice, one *need*. I couldn't imagine a world that didn't have you in it." She eased up on her tiptoes and brushed a kiss on his jaw.

With a growl, he lowered his head and captured her lips, so petal soft, in a full kiss. She clutched the borrowed T-shirt he wore and without another word, he lifted her up in his arms and carried her to his room. His shoulder hurt like hell, but he couldn't find it in him to care.

His mate was in his arms, she loved him, and her love was healing them both. He laid her on his bed and stripped out of his clothing before pulling her sweats and sweatshirt off. When he climbed onto the bed after her, she pushed him onto his back. He wanted to protest, but she nipped his throat playfully in a warning that he should stay where he lay. He surrendered, letting her cover his chest with kisses and then moved over the rest of his body. He closed his eyes and threw his head back, and she took his cock in her mouth.

"Fuck … that feels … incredible." He reached above his head and dug his fingers into the wood of the headboard, clawing at its clean surface.

His little mate chuckled before licking him, and he lost count of her sweet tortures. When she finally released him and he opened his eyes, he watched her climb on top of him to fully straddle him. Her beautiful bare breasts called for his touch, and he reached up, placing his palms around the mounds and lightly squeezing. Hadlee moaned at his exploring touching and lifted her hips, gently grasped his shaft, and guided him into her body. She welcomed him deep into her wet heat that tightened around him, and they both groaned together.

"You feel incredible," Indiana breathed, his voice low and gruff as he struggled to stay in control.

"So do you." She wriggled onto him, torturing them both with a riot of new sensations. He could feel her pleasure, feel it colliding with his own, like twin stars in a galaxy spiraling closer and closer, a collision of bright glorious explosions eminent.

"Ride me hard," he demanded, his hands grasping her hips. He was driven by a need to claim her, to make love to her so thoroughly to confirm they'd both survived something truly awful, and they were both alive. He wanted to erase her fear and her pain with his love. A true mate's love could heal almost anything.

"Yes," she rasped and started to move on him. He used his hold on her hips to make each thrust grind up against her and she made soft, desperate, mewling sounds as she came apart above him. A moment later, she slumped over on his chest. Indiana kissed her hair and rolled her beneath him as he stayed buried in her tight heat.

"Hold on, honey," he warned, and he moved wildly, surging deep. She gasped, her still-sensitive channel clinching down around his cock as he started a hard, fast, and almost brutal rhythm. He was so close, so damn close.

"More," she begged. "Give it to me," Hadlee demanded, a hint of her new bear layered in her growl. The excitement of that, of her and her bear wanting him and his bear was all he needed. He kissed her ruthlessly, his mouth seeking dominion as his body claimed hers and they came together, their pleasure springing into an explosion, bursting like a new star in the night sky of their shared world. Nothing ever felt like this. A unity of heart, mind, soul, and body.

"I love you, Indiana," Hadlee murmured as he feathered kisses on her jaw, her cheeks, her forehead.

He would worship her for as long as she'd let him. He was no longer a bear alone in the woods. He had his one true mate.

"Sorry you had to kill to save me," he whispered as he cuddled her close, their bodies still joined. He wouldn't have wished the burden of taking a life on anyone, especially not his woman, his mate, his love.

"You killed to save me, and you didn't even know me then," she replied. Her slumberous eyes moved over his face as she studied him.

Indiana nuzzled her temple with his nose before settling her even closer against his body.

"And I would kill again to protect you from danger," Indiana vowed.

"My bear ... she knew by the smell of those humans that they were dangerous. How could she know that?" Hadlee snuggled closer to him, and he cherished her need to be close. He had his own woman to hold, to cherish, to love with every fiber of his being. What a gift she truly was. It took him a moment to gather his feelings before he answered her question.

"Animals sense things humans have long since forgotten. When humans left the wild for their civilizations, they left those extra senses behind. Your bear still has them, so trust her. Her judgment will be sound."

"I have a *thousand* questions." She laughed softly. "But tonight I just want to sleep in your arms."

He smiled as he withdrew from her body, and pulled the covers back on the bed. They got under the sheets and he tucked her once more against his side. She would sleep in his arms. Tomorrow they would talk of the wild and the nature of bears.

Tomorrow.

What a beautiful word tomorrow was. It held the power to shine light upon every shadow in his soul. Tomorrow was a promise he would never dread again. Because he had his mate, *his love* in his arms. Two souls made one, two hearts beating in unison. Two bears roaming the wild, wonderful world. They were not alone; they had found each other and now the world held every dream within their reach.

"You can do this," Indiana encouraged.

Hadlee stared at Indiana from across the clearing, trying not to ogle too openly at his naked body. She was naked too, but he was obviously far more comfortable in his skin than she was. And damn if that wasn't distracting to see those gorgeous muscles and his broad shoulders and slender waist. It brought back far too tempting memories from that morning of how she'd had her legs wrapped around those hips as he'd taken her in the shower over and over until she'd been too tired and tender to walk. She bit her lip to keep from grinning.

"Hadlee, focus. I can hear your thoughts, remember?" Indiana didn't sound mad at all. Given the way lust heated his brown eyes like honey, he was definitely seeing her memories of their lovemaking play along the invisible bond between them.

"Sorry." She wasn't sorry at all.

She thought she would hate having access to his thoughts and he to hers, but it was better than she could have imagined. The connection between them wasn't irritating. She didn't hear every thought of his, just the ones he felt strongly about, the ones he seemed to desire to send to her, and vice versa. It was strangely freeing. It reminded her of when she'd been a child and she and her childhood friend across the street had walkie talkies. They'd talk to each other whenever they wanted. It was like having access to her best friend whenever she wanted to talk to him, even if he wasn't in the room. Their connection could spread at least thirty miles, possibly even farther, but she hadn't wanted to leave him to see how far she could really go.

With a sigh she made herself focus on what she was here to do. To change back into her bear.

"What if I attack you or Jones after I change?" She shot a glance at the dog, who lay sprawled in the grass. His tongue rolled out of his mouth as he happily watched the two humans as if this was an entirely normal sequence of events. Indiana had carried him for most of the hike, and now Jones was enjoying the shade of the nearby trees.

"You won't attack us. Bears aren't prone to attack by nature," his lips twitched as though he fought off a grin. "More often than not they turn and run."

"Except polar bears, they're supposed to be deadly," Hadlee added stubbornly. She had been reading every book she could in the last few weeks about bears while Indiana and Jones healed. Indiana had thought it sweet that she wanted to know everything about bears, but Hadlee wanted to be prepared. One of the ways she felt she was in control of herself was by researching the issue thoroughly.

"Honey." Indiana's chuckle was full of amusement. "You're *not* a polar bear. You're a brown bear. Now stop stalling and change."

He was right. She needed to stop looking and just jump.

Hadlee closed her eyes, let out a breath, and did what she had been practicing in her mind for weeks. She listened to the wilderness around her. The birch trees hummed in a strange but wonderful sort of rhythm. The mountains grumbled and the stream seemed to laugh in delight. Each piece of nature had its own sound, its own melody. All she had to do was find her own melody within it and answer the call of the bear's song.

The bear's song was like plucking invisible

vibrating strings out of the air. She reached for one strand that sang louder than the rest. It felt like a trumpet call to lead her home. In her mind she grasped that shimmering, gossamer strand and pulled it toward her. The bear came forth as easily as letting out one breath and drawing in another.

Joy filled her, like the warm sunshine on a chilly day. It covered every inch of her soul and burst outward in a solar flare. The bear was free and so was she. Smells filled her nose, and the breeze tickled her fur. She stretched her claws out, sinking them deep into the cool soil. And there it was, that easy sense of peace that came with choosing nature and its quiet magic into her heart.

She smelled Indiana and the dog. Her bear was used to them now, even though her bear had not been allowed out since that awful night. Hadlee had been practicing with Indiana's guidance to listen to her bear's thoughts over the last few weeks. Her bear didn't want to think about the past, her bear preferred to look forward. And for that Hadlee was grateful. She looked back enough on her own past; she didn't want her bear to dwell on it.

Hadlee ambled toward the human male who stood still, grinning at her.

"You're beautiful," he murmured as he held out a

hand for her to smell. "Your fur is more russet colored, not grizzled like mine. You're a true brown bear." He stroked her neck and head, and she lowered her head into his touch. It felt so good to feel his fingers in her fur and her bear rumbled in delight.

"All right, my turn," he said. He stepped back and a moment later, a tall grizzly bear faced her. He was nearly a foot taller than her, his hump a little more defined and his fur shimmering with glints of silver at the edges. He licked her nose, making her huff with delight, and then he bumped her shoulder with his head lightly, enticing her to play. She nipped him back and he took off running across the clearing. Jones barked in excitement but stayed in the shade, content to watch the two bears play. Hadlee gave chase, enjoying the easy loping move of the bear. She'd always thought bears were big clumsy creatures, but she was surprised to realize how lightly and easily she moved and how her paws spread over the ground, giving her a firm footing even as she ran.

Indiana turned around and came back toward her.

Hadlee stood up on her hind legs and Indiana did the same, play fighting until they both wore each other out and collapsed in a pile to rest. She quickly learned that she loved to wrestle with him, loved how he let her push against him and eventually how he would pin her down and let her playfully kick and nip at him. In bed he let her play, and he could also be rough, but he never hurt her. He always seemed to know exactly what she wanted and needed, likely because of their mate connection. Being with him was always fun, always exciting. And there were times when he took her slowly, gently, with such devoted tenderness that tears of joy streamed down her face and he kissed them away. Their bond only heightened as they mated because they were able to sense and feel each other's desires and needs.

She burrowed into Indiana's side and rested her head on her paws. He licked the fur on the top of her head in what she was learning was a bear's equivalent to when Indiana kissed the crown of her hair. She let out a rumbling sound of pure delight and dozed off in the early afternoon sunlight.

Hadlee woke sometime later to find she'd changed in her sleep to human again. Indiana was carrying her in his arms back to the large picnic blanket they had laid out earlier. He set her down on it, and she yawned as she stretched languidly. She was a little less bothered by her nakedness now. Her bear was unashamed of fur and skin, and it helped her feel less embarrassed.

"That was easy, wasn't it?" he asked her as he lay down beside her. He stroked a hand down her arm, then her hip, tracing invisible patterns with gentle fingertips.

"It was," she agreed. "I don't suppose every day will be this perfect?" she asked, knowing the answer before he spoke. She couldn't help but trace the scars along his face and want to kiss them.

"Not always, but we will try every day to find our glimmers."

"Glimmers?"

"Hmmm." He bent his head to nuzzle her before kissing her softly, sweetly. "Glimmers are those little moments of beautiful life that can come in the midst of the most mundane days. It might be the butterfly hovering above the flowers, or the smell of coming rain with the leaves rustling in the breeze. Whatever those small moments are, you must cling to them. Life, if we listen, will remind us how to live with joy and purpose."

Hadlee's heart tightened with a flood of love for this man. "How did you become so wise?" She was only half-teasing.

"Because I fell in love with you," he said simply, as if those words held every answer. Perhaps they did. For the last two months, she had been able to handle all the monumental life changes because she loved this man deeply. She'd quit her job, created her own marketing agency, and took Indiana's website design company as her first client. She had hired movers to pack up her apartment and drive her belongings from Chicago to Aspen Falls. She'd turned her mind and her heart toward life in the woods with the man she loved and their adorable dog Jones.

She knew they would face struggles, and there would always be a level of danger being bear shifters. But Wade, the sheriff, was on their side. He was a friend and ally. They took care to be safe, climbing into the higher lands of the mountains before changing into their bears.

Hadlee reslished all these changes in her life with a glad heart because she and Indiana were a *team*, a true set of partners in all ways. It was easier to make changes and sacrifices when she wasn't alone. That was something she had learned was different with Indiana compared to her life with her ex. Before Indy, she'd bent over backward and changed everything about herself to please her boyfriend while he'd done nothing to change himself. But with Indiana, it was a two-way street of changing and adapting to one another so they both found the same level of happiness together.

"What are you thinking about?" Indiana asked as she traced her fingertips over his chin and lips. His golden-brown eyes were hot with desire but tempered with patient love for her.

"I was thinking about how strange it is that my life led to this. That one walk in the woods managed to put me on the path to the right person." She hated that her voice trembled, but Indiana offered only warmth and understanding through their bond.

"True mates have a way of finding one another," Indiana said. "When I spoke to Dane yesterday, he told me he's heard stories of mates traveling halfway across the world by chance or because of some vague feeling, to find themselves in front of their possible true mates. It was as though when I went into the woods that day, the earth itself was guiding me toward you, to find you and save you. I believe fate brought us together in the same way."

"Fate and perhaps a bit of magic," she agreed.

"You love the idea of magic, don't you?" he teased, and stole a longer, deeper kiss from her.

"Yes I do. Because *nature* is magic. From the mushrooms that grow to the hawks flying above our heads. There is magic in everything in universe." The *immensity* of what she felt, that magic was born of love and nature, in that moment escaped the right words, but she felt it so clearly, so deeply, especially when she was in her bear form.

She knew she still had so much healing to do. Chad's attack had left her with nightmares and a few scars inside and out, but every day she was alive and striving for joy, was proof of her strength.

Indiana's lips curved as he gazed down at her. "I know the hike was one of the worst days of your life, but that was the day you saved *my* life." He leaned over to kiss her and cover her with his body. She embraced him, smoothing her hands over his bronzed back. She fell into his heady daze of sensual hunger as the trees sang all around them. They whispered a new song now, one that would travel with the northern winds to places far and away.

Once upon a time ... there was a woman who faced a choice between a man and a bear in the woods. She chose the bear ... she became the bear.

DID YOU LOVE STEPPING INTO THE WILD? THERE WILL BE **future stories in this series! So stay tuned and sign up for my newsletter HERE!**

THANK YOU!

Thank you so much for reading *Choose the Bear*! Now that you've finished the story I have to share with you where the inspiration for my hero and his dog came from. As I'm sure you noticed, Indy is named after the famous movie character Indiana Jones. I've always wanted to write a hero into a story named Indiana and this was my chance.

I discovered that George Lucas (one of the writers and executive producers of Indiana Jones) had dreamed up the name for the beloved archeologist because his large dog at the time was named Indiana, hence the origin story of the joke where Sean Connery teases Indiana Jones by saying "We named the dog, Indiana" in the movie. What struck me as delightful was watching an interview with George where he shows his dog and explains that he was a "big bear" of a dog. I thought it was absolutely perfect to have Indiana (my bear) and his dog Jones (the lovable mutt) as a tribute to a hero who always does the right thing, even at great cost.

If you loved this story, please feel free to share the cover or pull quotes or screenshots from the book on social media! I'm always delighted too see when readers find a story that resonates with them. Word of mouth between readers is still the best way for new readers to discover good books!

ABOUT THE AUTHOR

Lauren Smith is an Oklahoma attorney by day, author by night who pens adventurous and edgy romance stories by the light of her smart phone flashlight app. She knew she was destined to be a romance writer when she attempted to re-write the entire *Titanic* movie just to save Jack from drowning. Connecting with readers by writing emotionally moving, realistic and sexy romances no matter what time period is her passion. She's won multiple awards in several romance subgenres including: New England Reader's Choice Awards, Greater Detroit BookSeller's Best Awards, and a Semi-Finalist award for the Mary Wollstonecraft Shelley Award.

To Connect with Lauren, visit her at:
www.laurensmithbooks.com
lauren@laurensmithbooks.com

facebook.com/LaurenDianaSmith

x.com/LSmithAuthor

instagram.com/Laurensmithbooks

bookbub.com/authors/lauren-smith

tiktok.com/@laurenandemmabooks